The Magic Cottage

Book One:
The Velvet Bag Memoirs

By Hannah Greer
Illustrations by Tica Greer

PublishAmerica
Baltimore

ISBN: 1-60672-190-9
PUBLISHED BY PUBLISHAMERICA, LLLP
www.publishamerica.com
Baltimore

Printed in the United States of America

Dedication

This book is dedicated to all children
Who have touched my life with their passion for learning
Who made the world a better place because they dared to ask, "Why?"
Who never gave up the battle to prove that learning is fun
Who have never been afraid to take three steps forward and one step back
Who never stopped believing that everyday begins a new adventure
Who have the courage to say in a high tech world that books are the roadmaps to fantasy.

This book is especially dedicated to my supportive family, who believed in me when I found it difficult to believe in myself:
My husband of 35 years, Alan
My beautiful, creative daughter who has become a fabulous mother and wife, Mandy
My handsome son-in-law who makes parenting look easy and who shares his love with the world, Phinney
My son who has never stopped reaching for the stars and loves a good battle, Adam
And especially to my darling grandchildren—the inspiration of this book:
P.J. and Arliss

Acknowledgements

There are so many people to thank; special human beings who played the part of cheerleader when I began a new career at a turning point in my life. My family whom I already mentioned have stood by me through thick and thin. My sister, Tica, the illustrator of *The Magic Cottage*, and my special genie who told me a new story every night of my life until she married. My brother Frank who helped me edit the story, and my sister-in-law Sue whose photographic genius portrayed me as a young woman I think I am. I must also thank my two darling grand-nieces, Ryan and Madison who scrutinized every word and demonstrated the worth of this book as an educational tool with their many questions and their desire to write their own novel.

And my extended family who saw me through every edit: Margo Lindenmayer who sent me regular emails in which she provided insights into the characters; Dr. Glen Havens who saw talent in me before I saw it in myself and who made me promise to never give up; Sheryl Robertson who fed my spirit when my guardian angels seemed to have deserted me.

Chapter One
Finding Serendipity

"Higher!" Prentiss screeched, "I want to touch the Sunflower Queen!"

Asa gazed at his twin sister with a mixture of pride and amazement. "What an imagination," he thought, "She's always describing things as animals or plants." He pumped his legs as fast as he could, trying to reach the sun for his sibling. "Okay, here we go! Catch the sun ...er... I mean Marigold Queen in the sky if you can! And move over! You're hogging the swing!"

Prentiss looked at her brother with love in her heart and devilishness in her mind. "First, Asa, it doesn't look like a marigold. The sun looks like a beautiful Sunflower Queen this morning! Marigolds are nice, but sunflowers have specks of bright colors that pop out of the beautiful yellow petals, just like the queen sun up in the sky. Her kingdom is this whole meadow. And second, I am not hogging the swing. If you would've made it a little bigger, we would both fit on nicely. Besides, it's not a swing – it's our transporter!"

"Transporter? What's that... some kind of time machine?" questioned Asa.

"A transporter, little brother, is an imagination machine. Anyone knows that! Just try using your imagination, will you? You just have to think things up in your mind and the transporter will take you to the magic place. But," added Prentiss, "It only works here on top of this hill at Grammy and Papa's house. And it's our secret. No one else could possibly join us in the transporter. It's just ours for the summer while we're visiting Grammy and Papa. So don't talk about it to anyone else. Got it?"

**"A transporter, little brother, is an imagination machine.
Anyone knows that! Just try using your imagination, will you?"**

"Oh, I see, you think I'll spill the beans? You're the one who always gabs and tells secrets!" Asa teasingly smirked with a tinge of excitement at the thought of the kind of imaginative adventures he could unfold with his big sister's help.

"I do not! Who told mom about her surprise party that dad was planning last winter, huh?" Prentiss replied indignantly.

"Okay, whatever! We don't have time to fight! Let's call a truce!" Asa pleaded. Asa was much taller than Prentiss even though she was twenty-three minutes older, a fact his sister never let him forget. The twins shared a special bond that they believe began when they were in their mother's womb over eight years ago. Even though they fought like all siblings, the brother and sister could sense each other's feelings and vowed to protect each other from harm. They experienced many special friendships with other kids their age, but no one could break the unique attachment they had for each other.

The month they spent at Papa and Grammy's house each summer was filled with excitement, even though there were no computers, no televisions, no radios, and no electronic toys. Grammy told them in her melodic voice at the beginning of their stay each year, "The world is your classroom. Explore every inch and you will discover new things. Let your imaginations guide you, my darling grandchildren. If you don't exercise them, they will dry up and disappear. Then you will become shriveled up old folks."

Prentiss shuddered at the thought of a bunch of old wrinkled prune people rocking back and forth on porches with nothing to say or do. She wanted to stay young like Grammy. Even though she was really old – sixty-three – she looked much, much younger. She had baby soft skin and Prentiss loved to rub her hands against Grammy's long, slender fingers. The grandmother had chocolate brown eyes that sparkled with golden specks. Prentiss believed the specks were really fairy dust and that her grandmother had some pixie blood in her. Her soft chestnut hair—streaked with spun gold and a bit of silver—fell in waves to her shoulders. But it wasn't just her looks that made her seem young. Grammy loved to play with Asa and Prentiss more than anything else. She was more fun than any electronics!! In fact, she was more fun than any of the eight-year-olds Prentiss knew. Asa absorbed every word. He couldn't wait to research the countryside adjacent to Papa and Grammy's house. Asa loved to build things and Papa was always there to help with his tool shed filled with many interesting contraptions. Papa was forever willing to build something new. He always had time for his grandchildren. Asa looked lovingly at both grandparents. Papa was as jolly as Santa Claus, with a constant sparkle in his eyes and smile on his ruddy face. The grandfather had jet black hair that mysteriously had no sign of gray and always stayed exactly in place, as if each strand was glued to his head. Asa was sure that his grandmother, whose brown saucer eyes twinkled as she spoke, was a genie with special powers. She had a way of making every task fun. Ironing wasn't a chore, but a special event that turned clothing into jewels. Dusting had to be accomplished carefully so that the duster did not disturb the pixies that lived in castles on each microscopic particle.

He gazed at his sister absorbing every one of Grammy's words. He knew that Prentiss would anxiously want to leave the cozy haven of their grandparents' country home and begin this summer's adventures. The brother had to admit that he was excited about the possibilities that awaited them. He looked at his grandfather with admiration as the seventy-three-year-old formed a childish grin knowing that his grandchildren were in for a summer filled with fantasy and excitement.

Papa was the great organizer. "Keep everything in its proper place so that you don't lose one second of your dreams. And remember, Asa and Prentiss, that we share the earth with many other living things. Respect each one's space. We don't have a right to destroy anything for our own enjoyment. You can have an enjoyable life without turning things to rubble."

Asa's reminiscing about the conversations of the morning was interrupted by Prentiss.

"Asa, you stopped pumping. Come on! How are we ever going to transport ourselves into a new adventure if you poop out?"

"Okay! I was just thinking about what Papa said this morning. We have to respect nature around us. Do you think the swing—I mean transporter – is hurting the branch of this old tree?"

"No, of course not. We didn't cut any parts off or hammer nails into the bark. The wood planks were on the ground. So were the ropes and vines. I think this old tree likes our transporter!" added Prentiss. "So, come on! Think! Remember that we have to be home before dark!"

"I know, Prentiss. So we only have eight hours to transport ourselves," Asa added sarcastically.

"Eight hours isn't long when you go to new worlds," huffed Prentiss.

"Okay, okay. So what should we do first?" asked Asa. "We could pretend that we've landed, right?"

"Well, if we've landed we need to build our home first, just like any pioneers. When you explore new worlds, you have to worry about food and shelter first," remarked Prentiss.

"Well, Papa packed us enough food to last for a week," Asa chortled. "You know he always wants us prepared for any predicament." Asa scrounged through the neatly organized picnic basket of food: peanut butter and jelly sandwiches cut into animal shapes; fresh apples and bananas; homemade trail mix filled with nuts, berries, granola and oats; cut up fresh carrots and celery that reminded Asa of swords; and bottles of clear spring water.

"Right. So we have our special power food. Then we need shelter. Look around for a place we can build a shelter without disturbing the flora and fauna."

"Come on, Prentiss! We're on vacation so cut the scientific talk. Flora and fauna!! Can't you just say plants and animals?" begged Asa.

"We're explorers, Ace." Prentiss knew she would hit a soft spot in her brother's heart by using her special nickname for him. "We're scientists investigating new worlds. Flora and fauna work just fine. And remember what Grammy said, 'The world is our classroom.'"

"Okay. So let's get busy building over there, on the top of the hill." Asa was good at finding the perfect locations for the twins' adventures. Prentiss explored the spot her brother pointed out with her inquisitive emerald eyes. The hill was perfect: blanketed in velvety green grass, surrounded by old trees, and trimmed in rainbow colored wildflowers that framed the hill. To the east of the spot was a small pond the color of the turquoise in Grammy's favorite ring. North of the hill stood mighty groves of trees bursting with summer fruit.

"Oh, Asa, this is a perfect spot for our home in Serendipity!" Prentiss cried out with excitement.

"Sara dipped in tea? What?" asked Asa, knowing his intentional play on the words would drive his sister mad.

"Serendipity!" shouted Prentiss. "Don't be such a dope! Serendipity... isn't that perfect, Asa?"

"Not bad, Pren. Isn't serendipity a word that means finding something valuable by accident?"

"Exactly... And this is what this spot is... beautiful, valuable, and found by accident in our transporter! Wow, you do remember your vocabulary words, don't you? So you're not a complete imbecile!"

Asa blushed with embarrassment at his sister's half-compliment. Grammy had one requirement for their summer plans. The twins had to learn one new word each day. Fortunately, Grammy had a way of making learning fun. She would hide the new words under their pillows or write them on the bathroom mirror in toothpaste. Over breakfast, Asa and Prentiss would try to guess the meaning of the new word, with the help of Grammy and Papa who would give their grandchildren countless hints. Once learned, the twins both had a knack for remembering the new words forever; a gift that gave each of them a much larger vocabulary than any of the other kids in second grade last year.

A cool breeze on his face brought Asa back to the present. "Okay! Let's get started on building our shelter."

The twins jumped off the swing simultaneously. They seemed to be in perfect synchronization with each other – completing tasks at the same time. They explored the ground looking for things that could work for shelter without disturbing the inhabitants of Serendipity.

"Prentiss, I see what we can use! Look at those boulders near the pond. They're heavy and look kind of like the granite countertops in our kitchen at home. I don't think the creatures of Serendipity would mind if we move a few to build ourselves a cottage," explained Asa.

"Great! And we can use the old tree limbs lying around for the walls on top of the rock foundation and for the roof of course," squealed Prentiss with excitement bubbling from every pore.

Asa and Prentiss worked hard for hours dragging boulders to the top of the hill and piling dead tree limbs on top of them. When they were satisfied with the shelter they had formed, the children crawled into the middle of their creation, dragging their basket of food with them. They sat and talked for a long time, leisurely enjoying the feast Papa had provided for them. After awhile, the children fell fast asleep.

Asa awoke from a soothing nap first. He blinked hard as his green eyes stared at his surroundings. He gasped so loudly that he disturbed the dream-filled sleep of his sister. Prentiss sat up with a start, expecting to encounter the darkness formed by the twigs and stones surrounding her. She grabbed her brother's arm as she digested what she saw. "Ace, I-I-I think I am dreaming. If I tell you what I see, do you promise not to make fun of me?"

Asa answered in a hoarse whisper, "Pren, I'm having some kind of illusions myself! The twigs and rocks… well they've turned into a cottage!"

"Pren, I'm having some kind of illusions myself! The twigs and rocks… well they've turned into a cottage!"

Prentiss sighed with relief and excitement, "I see it too! Could we be having the same dream?"

"No, Pren. This is no dream… this is Serendipity and we're in the cottage we built with our own hands."

The twins took a few moments describing different parts of the cottage to assure they were imagining the same shelter. They agreed that the foundation of the small dwelling was formed from the granite colored black and gray speckled boulders. Atop the foundation rose walls of shingles the color of the brown twigs. A stone chimney formed to the right of the house. The crooked wooden steps led to a cozy porch complete with a red rocker and teal planter full of wildflowers. In the middle of the cottage stood a fine sturdy orange door. The two siblings discussed how much their father would like the orange door, as it was his favorite color. To the left of the front door, the children saw beautiful dark green shutters and below them a long orange planter filled with more wildflowers. Above the shutters a half-moon shaped window gave a peek at the interior, filled with a luminous yellow glow, the color of marigolds. Emerald green trim completed the lovely, small cottage. Prentiss and Asa wondered what they should do next.

"You think we should go in?" questioned Prentiss. "Do you think it's safe?"

Asa answered, "Well, I don't know. But it's our creation...I mean we imagined it. So I guess we can go in. What could happen?" The boy shuddered as he thought of all the horrible things that could be waiting for them inside. He tried to convince himself as well as his sister that everything would be okay, "It belongs to us. And besides, it looks so cozy inside. Look at the yellow light coming from that window. I bet there's furniture inside and everything we need. Come on, Pren. There's no turning back now. Besides, since this is our combined imagination at work, if we want to add something to our magic cottage we can, can't we?"

Prentiss thought for a moment. "Well, I guess you're right, Asa. But before we go in, just as a precaution, let's imagine a fence and a gate to protect us from any flora or fauna that may be dangerous. After all, Serendipity is just beginning to exist for us. With your imagination, who knows what scary creatures may pop up?"

The twins placed more stones leading down from the bottom of the front stairs to the bottom of the hill. At the edge, they placed dead tree limbs equally spaced to form a fine fence. They even imagined a gate to assure their protection from outside visitors. Asa and Prentiss closed their eyes. When they reopened them, the tasks had been completed. A sturdy brown fence surrounded the house, complimented by a fine gate decorated with wildflowers and vines. After gazing admiringly at their creations, the two turned to face the front door of their cottage. Holding the remains of their packed lunch, Asa led the way up the stairs to the front door. Just as they reached the top step, brother and sister heard some strange noises coming from within the dwelling.

"Did you hear that?" whispered Prentiss.

"Yeah!" answered Asa nervously. "You know, it's getting kind of late. Maybe we better get in the transporter and return home. Tomorrow, we can come back to Serendipity and the magic cottage when we have more supplies." He was hoping his sister would agree with him, so that he would not appear frightened to go into their cottage. Asa was relieved when Prentiss spoke.

"Good plan, Ace. Let's go home!" Prentiss led the way down the steps.

After riding on the transporter for a few moments, the twins jumped off and ran all the way back to Grammy and Papa's house. Their imaginations were exhausted for the day. They knew after a good night's rest they would be ready for more adventures in Serendipity. But for the moment, they were happy to feel snug under the old comforters that layered their iron-framed beds in their grandparents' house. The children were comforted by their grandparents' bear hugs and butterfly kisses.

Grammy stood at the bedroom door watching over her beloved grandchildren as they fell into a deep sleep. She knew her daughter's children eagerly soaked up everything Papa and she said. She studied Asa and Prentiss's faces, combinations of their mother's and father's genes. She marveled at the fact that both children had their father's emerald green eyes that exploded with the hues of nature. They also had his chestnut brown hair that glistened with flecks of spun gold and crimson rubies. Their smiles came from their mother… a bit crooked as their lips dipped to one side, giving them a mixture of angelic and devilish expressions.

But Grammy thought with a sense of pride that their love for imagining new worlds came from her. It was her goal to see that the children stretched their imaginations each summer and developed a love for learning that would carry them through the rest of their lives. She knew the whimsical trips they imagined would prepare them for the truth about their heritage. They would learn in good time the magical bloodline that graced the family. They would be told the history of the land on which Grammy and Papa lived now and where their ancestors also resided; a lineage dating back thousands of years whose secrets were kept securely hidden in beautifully detailed velvet bags in the upstairs attic and known to the elders in each generation as The Velvet Bag Memoirs. But this summer, the eight-year-olds would begin their preparation for the future through the expansion of their beautiful imaginations.

The children dreamed of Serendipity and imagined what exciting adventures awaited them. The twins especially wanted to investigate the strange noises coming from within their magic cottage. Together they would find the courage to overcome fear of the unknown.

Chapter Two
Sherlock and Nikki

Morning came quickly for the twins. They soaked in the warmth of the Sunflower Queen's rays as they watched Papa lovingly pack new supplies for another adventure in Serendipity. They said good-bye to Papa and Grammy, gave each bear hugs and butterfly kisses and sprinted up the hill to their transporter. Pumping their legs in perfect harmony, Asa and Prentiss soared high into the sky, almost touching the cotton ball fluffy clouds. After a few moments, the twins were back in Serendipity, standing in front of the magic cottage.

To their amazement and relief, the cottage was still there. They leaped up the wooden steps and stopped for a moment to ride the red rocker that still stood on the porch. Prentiss checked the wildflowers in the planters to see if they needed water. Asa was anxious about going inside the cottage but swallowed his fear and said, "Well, Pren, don't you think it's time we went inside?"

Prentiss was also anxious and felt her kneecaps twitching. "Sure. Let's see what our imaginations have cooked up."

The twins faced the orange door. Just at that moment, they heard a faint scratching noise just like the sound they heard the day before. "Did you hear that?" whispered Prentiss.

"Yes, I did," answered Asa. "Remember, any fauna or flora we create comes from our own brains."

Just at that moment, a familiar bark greeted the twins' ears. The two grinned at each other with a mutual understanding of what creature their minds had created inside the cottage.

"I'd know that bark anywhere," chuckled Asa with relief. "That's our good old dog, Nikki."

At the mention of her name, Nikki barked even louder than before.

"You're right!" Prentiss squealed with excitement. She reached for the front doorknob and quickly opened the door. Sitting on a beautifully braided oval blue rug stood the twins' best friend, their dog Nikki. Asa and Prentiss were not quite sure how their imaginations had transported their household pet from their home to Serendipity, but they were very glad to see her. Nikki was a great dog. She did not have any pedigrees; in fact she was a mixed breed – part Labrador and part something else—but she was smart, obedient, and full of love for her twin masters. Nikki's brick red fur glistened in the glow of the marigold light coming from within the cottage.

Sitting on a beautifully braided oval blue rug stood the twins' best friend, their dog Nikki.

Prentiss and Asa almost knocked the dog over, embracing her with their strong sun-browned arms. Nikki returned the welcome with very wet licks of her tongue across the smiling faces of the brother and sister. The dog continued barking a welcome greeting to the children, when something miraculous happened. All of the sudden the barks became words. Nikki was speaking to the twins in English! In utter amazement, Prentiss and Asa stared at each other, blinked their green eyes, swallowed hard, and acknowledged to each other that they were both hearing the same words from their trusted canine companion.

Nikki immediately understood that the humans were surprised. "Don't be shocked," she barked in English. "When you transported me to Serendipity, you also gave me the ability to speak English. You know that I already had quite a good understanding of your language. You two always marvel when I go fetch my favorite ball or play tag with you, just by your asking me. But I know a lot of words. I started understanding when I was just a pup." Nikki looked around at her new surroundings with pride and said, "So, this is where I live. Nice job on the cottage! It's perfect! Would you like me to show you around?"

Prentiss and Asa got over their shock of their talking dog and followed Nikki on a tour of the cottage they had created from their incredible imaginations. There were only a few rooms but each one was quite large. To the right of the front door stood a large living area, complete with a huge fireplace that served as a stove as well as the only source of heat. Prentiss really imagined her brother and herself as pioneers living in a log cabin somewhere in the territory that would become the United States. The room was not crowded with furniture. Two overstuffed blue floral chairs stood on either side of the fireplace. A round mahogany table stood in the middle of the room surrounded by four wooden chairs, each constructed of a different wood. To the left of the front door Nikki showed the twins a huge bathroom complete with the largest bathtub Prentiss had ever seen. She dreamed of taking long bubble baths in the tub, sculpting animals out of the foamy suds. Asa must have imagined the shower that looked like a waterfall that stood adjacent to the tub. Since he was a baby, he loved dunking his head under the water, allowing streams of liquid to run down his face and neck. Two sinks and a toilet completed the bathroom. Behind this room a long hallway led to the back of the cottage. Two bedrooms stood side by side, each of equal size. Prentiss guessed the rooms were equal in area to keep Asa and her from fighting. Each bedroom looked identical: nice soft featherbeds, a desk and chair, and a long winding ladder leading up to lofts at the top. Wasting no time to climb his ladder, Asa discovered the half-moon shaped window taking up almost one wall of his loft. Flickering candles decorated the tables in each loft, explaining the marigold color light the twins saw from the porch.

Asa sighed, "This place is just perfect! I could live here forever!"

"It is nice," added Prentiss. "I just will think of the color I want my bedroom walls. I think purple would be nice. Yes, purple it is. And a purple floral bedspread, too." She blinked her eyes and her bedroom turned into a violet array of luxury. "Now, that's perfect!!"

Prentiss and Asa followed Nikki back to the entry way. Suddenly, Nikki froze into a hunting dog's pointer position. Prentiss asked, "What is it, Nikki?"

The dog growled back, "Shh! I'll explain in a moment. It's Sherlock up to his old tricks."

"Sherlock? Who's that?" asked Asa.

Nikki replied, "Please! Patience! I'll explain in a minute."

The twins were totally confused but obeyed their dog. They waited patiently for Nikki to explain. After a few minutes, Nikki turned to the children and said, "Okay. Slowly turn to the door and look outside towards those trees. Do you see an orange and yellow birdhouse?"

To their amazement, the birdhouse Nikki described now hung from a low branch of one of the trees adjacent to the cottage. "How did that get there?" questioned Asa.

Nikki answered, "Remember, everything in Serendipity comes from your imaginations. You put the birdhouse there. Now look on top of the birdhouse. Do you see a gray squirrel perched on the roof? Asa and Prentiss, meet Sherlock – the orneriest squirrel you will ever know. He spends his days leaving clues inside the birdhouse. Oh, not just on pieces of paper. Oh, no, that would be too easy. Sherlock pierces a tiny hole in the shell of an acorn and leaves clues on dried up leaves he carefully rolls up and puts inside the acorn shell. Sometimes it takes me five hours to get the clue out of the shell!! But the mystery prize is always worth trying to solve the problem."

**Asa and Prentiss, meet Sherlock – the orneriest squirrel
you will ever know.**

"Oh, I get it!" shouted Prentiss triumphantly. "Sherlock is for
Sherlock Holmes, the greatest detective ever at Scotland Yard."

"Yeah," added Asa. "That's perfect. Don't forget that Sherlock
Holmes was a fictitious character, not a real person. Remember,
Grammy told us all about him. He was the imagination of Sir Arthur
Conan Doyle. And somehow old Sherlock has come to live in
Serendipity in the form of a squirrel. Prentiss, I told you that reading
all those mysteries would get into your brain!"

"Hah! You're right, Ace. I guess Sherlock is my creation!" chuckled Prentiss. "So is he a good detective, Nikki?"

"It's more like he creates good detectives. You'll see what I mean. Just go get the acorn out of the birdhouse and we will see what old Sherlock is up to."

Asa and Prentiss leaped down the front stairs and ran to the birdhouse. Asa carefully put his hand inside the opening and pulled out an acorn the size of a baseball. It clearly had been gnawed on, because there was a hole on one end of the shell. Asa and Prentiss ran back to Nikki who was now rocking in the red chair on the porch.

Nikki directed Asa to carefully reach inside the acorn and pull out the message written on the leaf.

Asa said, "Wow, this is strange. It's a math problem. Oh, no!! More school work in the middle of summer!!"

Nikki barked softly, "Okay! Share the problem and let's see if putting our heads together, we can solve it!"

Asa read:

Add the stones from step to gate,
Subtract three and divide by eight.
The answer will give you the number true,
Of stones that hide a gift for you.
Face the cottage and start where the counting did end,
To get the clue you'll have to bend.
Larger than Nikki and black as coal,
Look under this one to find your goal.

"Why don't we just dig up each stone?" cried Prentiss excitedly.

"Because if you make a mistake," yelped Nikki, "the prize will disappear and so will Sherlock! You must think before you act!"

Asa, in his analytical way, had a plan. "Okay, let's take a line at a time. The first part is pretty clear. Start at the bottom step of the cottage and count the number of stones in the path until we get to the gate."

Prentiss questioned, "So, does that mean all the stones or just the ones we can truly see until we reach the gate?"

Asa replied, "Just to the gate. That's pretty clear. Pren, you count and I'll be backup."

Prentiss nodded and stood on the first stone next to the bottom step of the cottage. Carefully she stepped on each stone leading to the gate. The twins checked their totals several times, and they agreed that the number always equaled eleven.

"Okay, let's go with eleven. The next line says to subtract three. That's easy. Eleven minus three is eight. Then divide by eight. Eight divided by eight is one. So there is only one right stone! That's encouraging!" Asa added rolling his eyes.

"Don't be sarcastic, Ace," warned Prentiss. "That won't help anything! What's the next line?"

Asa read: "*Face the cottage and start where the counting did end; to get the clue you'll have to bend.* Okay, the counting ended at the gate. So turn around and face the cottage standing next to the gate. Now, bend down and what do you see, Pren?"

"Well, Ace," analyzed Prentiss, "It could be one of two stones, one gray and one black. But the last line says the stone is bigger than Nikki and very black. So, I guess it has to be this big black one. Do you two agree?"

Asa nodded his head and Nikki barked and wagged her tail. It was unanimous. Very carefully the twins wiped off the huge black stone. Nikki dug at it with her claws. Soon it was loose enough to lift. Asa raised the stone carefully while Prentiss looked underneath. To her surprise Prentiss pulled out a beautiful golden locket in the shape of a dazzling sunflower. She examined each pointy ray of the object until she discovered one that twisted and clicked. The locket popped open, revealing the smallest book the twins had ever seen. The title of the velvety black book was written in golden letters: *The Legend of Serendipity*. The book was so small that only one word was written on each ivory page. Altogether the letters formed these words:

"Do not fear to imagine. You are safe in the land of Serendipity where curiosity leads to exciting new adventures. The legend goes that those who learn from their experiences in Serendipity shall never grow old, but shall have the heart and mind of children and the wisdom of the wisest of souls all the rest of their days." It was signed, *The Sunflower Queen.*

The twins were so focused on the tiny book that they did not notice that Sherlock had joined the group, perched on top of Nikki's head. After everything that had happened in the past two days, Asa and Prentiss were not very surprised when the squirrel began speaking to them in perfect British English:

"Right! Well, congratulations, young yanks. Pretty keen for babes just out of their nappies! So glad you are spending your holiday with us. You figured out me clue and found quite a treasure. Serendipity does not get many visitors anymore. It seems children are more interested in sitting on couches playing electronic games all day. It's a pity, you know. Imaginations are rotting away. Your smart Grammy and Papa know the secret of a happy life and it begins with stretching those minds and creating new wonderment wherever you go. It is the way of never getting bored, don't you know?"

Asa asked, "Mr. Sherlock, sir, do you know our Papa and Grammy?"

The squirrel answered, "Aye, you can call me Sherlock, son. I know your Papa and Grammy well. I have played with them many times right here on this very hill. And your mum and dad, too. Now it is your turn. You will find more clues and meet more inhabitants of Serendipity. Your minds shall lead the way. Well, it is teatime you know. I will see you again, right?"

But before Prentiss or Asa could answer, Sherlock had scampered off across the stone path, over the wooden fence, and up the tree where the birdhouse stood. He disappeared into a hole right in the middle of the tree.

"What just happened?" cried Asa. "Everything moves so fast around here, I feel like I'm spinning. I need to sit down for a minute."

Asa began to lean against the gate, when Nikki barked, "Be careful where you lean, Asa. There are creatures everywhere in Serendipity. Mind their space."

Prentiss chirped in, "Do you mean that something lives in this gate, too? This is getting stranger by the minute." Examining the gate, Prentiss added, "Nikki, I don't see anything there. Are you sure that something is inside the gate?"

"Not inside the gate, Prentiss. On the gate. Yes, she's there now. She's just a bit shy but you will love the adventures she has in store for you."

"She?" asked Asa. "She who? I'm getting an awful headache. Where is this creature? Come out, come out wherever you are!" sang Asa.

"Shh!" scolded Nikki. "You're scaring her. Calm down, sit on the stones with your sister, and I'll try to coax her out for you!"

At that moment, Asa could hear Grammy's dinner bell far off in the distance. "I'm afraid we won't be able to meet any more of your friends today, Nikki. We have to get in the transporter and go home. We'll see you tomorrow."

"Well, all right," whined Nikki a bit disappointed. "I'll see you two bright and early tomorrow. Prentiss, you are in charge of the locket. Wear it always and keep it safe. The Sunflower Queen does not often give gifts; especially one as valuable as that locket. When you accepted it, you also took on the responsibility of keeping it safe. Well, have a good evening."

Prentiss had many questions about the locket. "Wait! Nikki, what does this locket do? Keep it safe from what? Why is it so valuable?"

But Nikki was in too much of a hurry to answer questions. "Not now, Prentiss. Tomorrow you will learn more. Just keep it safe!"

With that Nikki pranced up the stairs into the cottage and closed the bright orange door. Prentiss and Asa thought they heard something rustling in the vines that decorated the gate. But they still couldn't see anything. Their growling stomachs told them it was time to go back to Grammy and Papa's house. The twins could barely wait for tomorrow to come.

Chapter Three
Morph

The next day it didn't take long for Prentiss and Asa to finish their chores at their grandparents' house, grab the supplies Papa packed for them, and get back to the transporter. They were anxious to meet another inhabitant of Serendipity and see Sherlock and Nikki. The transporter ride was short and uneventful. The twins jumped off the vehicle as soon as it landed and sprinted up the hill to the cottage. Nikki was already waiting for them, swaying back and forth on the red rocker. Sherlock was perched on Nikki's head.

"Well, good morning, Asa and Prentiss!" barked Nikki. "I'm glad you made it back to Serendipity. We have been waiting for you."

"Top of the day to you!" added Sherlock. "I hope you had an absolutely scrumptious breakfast this morning. You are going to need all your brain cells today!"

Asa flinched at the idea that he would have more problems to solve. Prentiss giggled with excitement. She said, "So when do we meet who or what lives on the gate?"

"Patience is a virtue," Sherlock said lovingly. "But, all right. Move very quietly and tiptoe over to the gate. Tell me what you see."

Asa quickly answered, "Lots of wildflowers, vines like on our transporter, a rope to hold the gate closed, and… well, that's all!"

"Look again, boy," Sherlock directed. "Things are not always what they first appear to be, right?"

Asa squinted his eyes to focus on the gate but couldn't see anything unusual. Prentiss decided to take a long, hard look. She imagined she had a magnifying glass in her right hand. She did not realize that she squeezed the golden locket in her left hand with such force that it popped open. Prentiss was surprised when her thoughts became realities, for in her right hand she held a beautiful magnifying glass just like she had imagined. "Wow!" She whispered more to herself than any of her companions. "I better be careful about my thoughts!"

Prentiss used the magnifying glass to examine the gate carefully. Every detail appeared just as Asa had described. Suddenly, one of the purple flowers moved. Why it was a magnificent butterfly – her wings were the most beautiful shades of violet Prentiss had ever seen!

Why it was a magnificent butterfly – her wings were the most beautiful shades of violet Prentiss had ever seen!

In the softest whisper she could muster Prentiss greeted the butterfly, "Good morning, ma'am. I'm Prentiss and this is my brother Asa. We are new to Serendipity. We hope that we can be your new friends. We mean you no harm, really."

Worrying that the small, timid creature might think the magnifying glass was some kind of weapon, Prentiss placed it carefully in her pocket. The butterfly was startled by the human voice and flit away hovering in circles above the gate.

"It's okay," Nikki said reassuringly. "Morph is very shy, remember. She will have to get used to your voices and your giant size. But if you look on the gatepost, you will see that Morph has left you something in the mailbox."

"Here we go again," sighed Asa. "Wait, Nikki and Sherlock. Hold on a minute. First, what kind of a name is Morph? I don't remember that from school!!"

Sherlock replied, "Well, Asa, it is a nickname for Chrysalis Metamorphosis."

"I'm sorry I asked," laughed Asa. "If that's not a mouthful! Why that name is longer than she is!"

"With good reason," Sherlock answered. Looking very much like their second grade teacher, Mr. Rodney, Sherlock began his lecture. "A butterfly begins life as something quite different and –"

Asa interrupted, "That much I know… it starts as a caterpillar."

"Excellent, Asa," Sherlock continued with pride in his student's intellectual capacities. "Well, right, the caterpillar eats for awhile and then begins a journey unlike any other creature. It forms a chrysalis. Inside this cocoon, the caterpillar is changed into a completely different living creature. This magical change of nature is called metamorphosis. Other animals go through metamorphosis, but none as uniquely and completely as the butterfly."

"Oh, you mean like when tadpoles become frogs. Is that metamorphosis?" added Prentiss, not to be outdone by her brother.

"Perfect, miss!" Sherlock praised the young girl. "When the butterfly comes out of the chrysalis, it is very unique. No two are exactly the same, just like children, even twins. So you are looking at a very special gift of nature." Looking up at the beautiful violet butterfly, Sherlock coaxed, "Come on now, Morph. The children won't hurt you. They are very important people here in Serendipity. You do have something you want them to do, now don't you?"

Morph fluttered about and eventually landed on a green and orange mailbox that appeared atop the left gatepost. Asa said a bit too loudly, "And that's another thing! When did that mailbox get there?"

Nikki licked Asa's face adoringly, "It's been here all the time, Asa. You just couldn't see it before. Now, if you think you can keep your voice down so that you don't scare Morph to death, I believe she has something to share with you that is inside that mailbox."

Prentiss realized that Morph had not uttered one sound. "You two both talk English. Can't Morph speak?"

Sherlock retorted, "Well, I speak English anyway. I believe the rest of you speak that funny dialect, American!! Morph doesn't speak, but she does communicate. I believe the two of you have mail. Look inside the letter box, please."

Prentiss was getting used to this routine. Things appeared so fast in Serendipity and always with a purpose. She carefully stuck her hand inside the mailbox. She pulled out a small sheet of lace, as soft as the finest silk. Letters were written upon the gift, but Prentiss could not decipher their meaning.

Asa tried to grab the lace sheet from his sister's hand, but she was too fast. She had had eight years of practicing how to hang on to something that her brother wanted. Prentiss snapped at Asa, "Be careful, Ace. I'll show you in just a minute. Look at this now carefully. It is so fragile. What do the letters mean?" Prentiss carefully placed the lace sheet on one of the stones in the pathway.

The twins both stared at the letters for what seemed like hours:
bpplruelal

Asa was perplexed, "What is this? Don't tell me it's another problem?"

Sherlock shook his bushy tail with glee. "Why, yes, boy, so it is.

34

The problem is that the letters are jumbled up, scrambled. But I will also give you a clue. Go look in the birdhouse."

Asa ran over to the birdhouse and sure enough, he found another acorn inside. He carefully removed the message leaf inside and read to his sister, *"What is now one must become two."*

Asa and Prentiss thought about both mystery clues for what seemed like a long time. After a few minutes, Asa jumped up with excitement, "What is now one...one jumbled mess of letters must become two... two words. This isn't one word but two. Start unscrambling, Pren."

The twins scratched letters into the dirt that cemented the stone pathway together.

Blue appler
Blue rapple
Pure bplrlal
Bar ppluell
Purple albl

Prentiss and Asa rolled on the ground with laughter at the funny combinations they created. Prentiss then had an idea. "Look, Ace, at the last one."

"You mean the purple albl?" roared Asa.

"No, I mean a purple ball," Prentiss shouted triumphantly.

Nikki jumped in circles, wagging her tail. Sherlock twittered and said, "Congratulations! You have guessed it! My, you are becoming outstanding detectives!"

"Thank you," answered Asa, "but I don't see any purple ball." Before Sherlock or Nikki could answer, Asa added, "But I know... look around and one will pop up somewhere!!"

Nikki chimed in, "Follow Morph, follow Morph."

At that moment Chrysalis Metamorphosis was flying across the green meadow to a spot in front of the cottage where the grass grew in an odd striped green formation. There in the middle of the pattern, stood a beautiful purple ball. Prentiss ran to the location, hoping to outrun her brother and be the first to reach the purple sphere. Sherlock warned, "Not so fast, Prentiss. Listen carefully before grabbing at things. Patience ..."

"is a virtue..." Prentiss completed the phrase. "So what is going to happen?"

Nikki calmly explained, "You already know that everything in Serendipity is planned and everything has a purpose. Your imaginations are doing the planning and creating the purposes. This violet orb is quite special. It has the powers to make things larger or smaller than they really are. It can also make them move. This may come in quite handy at some point in your adventures in Serendipity. Morph wants you to be the keeper of the orb, Asa. So, lift it carefully and look to see what lies beneath it."

This violet orb is quite special. It has the powers to make things larger or smaller than they really are. It can also make them move.

Asa trembled with pride that this prize was his responsibility. He had to admit that he was a bit jealous yesterday when Prentiss was named keeper of the golden locket. Asa felt that things were evening out somewhat. The boy lifted the orb to discover a magnificent yellow truck underneath the ball. Asa has had a special fondness for trucks since he was just a baby. He circled the treasure several times, knowing something was about to happen. He thought to himself, "I wish this truck was the size of a real one so I could drive it all over Serendipity." Before he knew what had happened, the purple ball lifted into the sky and the yellow toy became a full-sized vehicle.

"Bravo! Go on! Jump on the lorry! Give it a whirl!" directed Sherlock.

"But I can't drive. I don't have a license for one thing and I'm only eight!" cried Asa.

"Oh, posh!" retorted Sherlock, "This is Serendipity. You can do what you want! Now get into the cab, turn on the ignition, and take your sister on a wild ride. Go ahead! Hit every pothole, fly over every bump! Speed in and out of those groves! Go, boy! Have the time of your life!!"

Without waiting for an invitation, Prentiss jumped into the passenger side of the cab. Asa found the key on the driver's side, started up the truck, and away they flew! Sherlock and Nikki could hear the twins laughing and screeching as they took the wildest ride of their young lives. Morph flew in circles, watching over the children like a guardian angel. Childhood giving way to common sense, Asa and Prentiss had a great time hitting bumps so hard that the two were airborne inside the cab for seconds at a time. When they felt the truck slowing down, they realized that it was driving them back to the meadow in front of the magic cottage. It stopped right in front of Sherlock and Nikki, just like a ride in an amusement park.

Nikki, always the protector of her humans warned, "My darlings, remember! Things like this adventure only occur here in your imaginations, in Serendipity. You must never drive recklessly at home… promise me… such danger is foolish and not allowed! Whenever you feel the devilish desire to let go of reason…do so where it is safe… here in Serendipity. Let your imaginations take you on such perilous rides. Do you understand?"

The children nodded with a newly found respect for their pet. They knew instinctively that she spoke the truth. They understood why she was an important part of Serendipity and why she lived in the magic cottage. Nikki was their protector and teacher. She would lead them through memories of a lifetime without allowing them to fall into harm's way. She would introduce them to new friends and take them on adventures that would live in the children's memories long into adulthood.

As soon as the children disembarked from the yellow truck, the vehicle shrank back to toy size. The purple orb rolled in front of the toy and stopped. Asa took charge of his prize, which shrank to the size of a quarter. He placed the violet ball in his pocket for safe keeping. The children were exhausted with the adventures of this day in Serendipity. They had successfully solved another puzzle, winning the much desired respect of Sherlock. They had met a new friend, Morph, who was so shy she would not speak. She proved to the twins that powerful deeds come in all shapes and sizes. Most of all, their love for their canine companion, Nikki, overflowed the twins' hearts. Prentiss and Asa could not wait to discover what new adventures lurked in the future. They only knew that it was time to return to Papa and Grammy's house. Their tired bodies barely exerted enough energy to pump the transporter back home.

As they walked down the path to their grandparents' house, the twins saw their grandmother beaming at them with her twinkling eyes. "How was your day, my sweet peas? Did you do anything interesting?"

"Oh, Grammy, we had so much fun racing…" Prentiss was cut off by a thwack on her head from her brother. She turned and sneered at him and then remembered how they were sworn to secrecy about their adventures in Serendipity. Prentiss continued more cautiously, "…racing around and doing this and that! How was your day?"

By that time, Papa had joined the group. "Oh, it was fine, fine! I spent the morning working on my yellow truck… it's been stalling. Then the darn thing just took off on its own and zoomed up the hill. You haven't seen it have you?"

Asa answered, "I don't think so, Papa. But that sure is strange! What are you going to do?"

Papa smiled, "Oh, not to worry. It will come back soon. I think it just wanted a joyride." Papa looked at Grammy and the grandparents smiled at each other and winked.

Asa and Prentiss stared at each other and wondered just how much their grandparents knew about their adventures. Prentiss fingered the beautiful golden locket she wore around her neck and added, "Very strange… very strange indeed!"

After a scrumptious dinner, Grammy read to the twins as she did every night. But Asa and Prentiss couldn't hide their amazement when she began to read, *The Adventures of Sherlock Holmes*, by Sir Arthur Conan Doyle. "What is it, my loves? Do you not like Sherlock anymore? Have you heard the stories too many times?"

"Oh, no, Grammy, we love Sherlock stories. He's one of our favorites! We love solving his clues!" Prentiss explained. But at the last words, Asa kicked her in the shin. Prentiss knew that she was giving away too much information. She scowled at her twin and then added, "You know, Grammy, we like to follow along in the story and see if we can solve the mysteries using the clues!"

The twins thought they saw Grammy and Papa wink at each other again, but they were too tired to think about the coincidences of the day with the yellow truck and Sherlock. That night the children slept more soundly than they ever had in their entire lives. They dreamed of new friends they would meet in Serendipity and could not wait to discover what parts they would play in their personal imagination world in the days to come.

Chapter Four
Herbie

The Sunflower Queen was just beginning to spread her rays for the morning's first light when Asa and Prentiss arrived in Serendipity. Asa checked his pocket as he jumped off the transporter to make sure he had remembered the purple ball. He was not going to seem irresponsible when Sherlock, Nikki, and Morph were depending on him to take care of the great treasure. He gave a sigh of relief as he felt the desired object sitting safely in his jean pocket. Simultaneously, Prentiss clutched the golden locket that hung snugly around her neck. She had similar thoughts as her brother and hoped that the Serendipity inhabitants would notice that she had responsibly worn the locket she had been awarded.

As the twins approached the gate that led up to the magic cottage front steps, the brother and sister noticed that none of their friends appeared to be around. Prentiss pulled out the magnifying glass to see if she could spot Morph, but she was nowhere to be found. The red rocker was stationary on the porch. The orange door to the cottage was closed. Just as Asa and Prentiss were about to unlatch the gate, they noticed something new hanging from an old rusty nail on one of the fence rails.

Asa said to his sister, "Pren, it looks like we cooked up something new for today. Looks like one of us was hungry for carrots. They do look good, don't they?"

The twins heard rustling behind the red bucket filled to the brim with carrots. Soon, a white furry head appeared. A nervous voice warned, "Tsk..tsk..tsk. Now don't you touch my carrots. I have been growing them for awhile, pruning away the weeds, watering them, and no humans – even ones as handsome and beautiful as the two of you – are going to snatch them from me. Why everyone knows rabbits are herbivores and carrots happen to be my favorite food."

A nervous voice warned, "Tsk..tsk..tsk. Now don't you
touch my carrots. I have been growing them for awhile,
pruning away the weeds, watering them, and no humans –
even ones as handsome and beautiful as the two of you –
are going to snatch them from me."

The creature had worked himself up into such a state that his hind leg kept thumping and rattling the mailbox. Neither Prentiss nor Asa had time to say a word during all this commotion. They stood there with their mouths gaping and their emerald eyes staring like four green melons.

When the rabbit began to calm down, the front door to the cottage opened and out came Morph, Nikki, and Sherlock.

Nikki pranced over to her humans to make sure they were okay. "Good morning! What is all the fuss?"

"Don't blame us, Nikki. We were minding our own business, looking around to see where all of you were and this rabbit started going bonkers. It thought we were going to steal its carrots."

The rabbit sputtered indignantly, "I was not going… as you say, young man, bonkers… I was protecting my property. As an upstanding citizen of Serendipity, I have a right to protect what is mine, mine, mine."

"Calm down, Herbie," soothed Sherlock. "No one is going to pinch your carrots. These are our new mates. Herbie Vore, let me introduce Asa and Prentiss Fallmark." It had been a long time since the twins heard their family name used. Asa wondered if this rabbit was a snooty kind of creature big on manners and formalities.

Herbie scratched his long ears with his large paw and mumbled, "Fallmark? Fallmark? It seems many years ago there was another human boy with that name! Didn't he wed the cute girl who played here too? Yes, yes… I made a carrot cake for their wedding! Think! Think! Think! Her name escapes me… oh… it's…"

Nikki jumped up on the rabbit and knocked him to the ground. Herbie screeched, "Hey! Is it a fight you want, you four legged good-for-nothing…"

Sherlock handled the situation. "Right, Herbie. I think you interrupted the twin's introductions. Let's not be rude, right?"

The twins stared at each other with confusion written all over their young faces. They decided to let the commotion go without comment. Prentiss picked up on the formal introductions that had been interrupted. Curtseying as low as she could, she held out her hand and said, "How do you do?"

Of course, Herbie worried about the girl's hand swiping some carrots and quickly jumped up on top of the red bucket. The black rope holding the bucket began to spin from the motion, making Herbie Vore twist in circles. After a few seconds, the rabbit fell off the bucket and onto his back right in the middle of the grass. He seemed to be a bit stunned, "Is it time to get up yet, Mom?"

Nikki licked Herbie's face and said, "Herbie, Herbie, are you okay? Answer me? Do you know where you are? Snap out of it!"

Herbie raised his head, twitched his nose, and said, "Huh? Where am I? Oh, hello, Nikki. How are you this morning?" Then the rabbit spotted the humans again. "Oh, no! They're still here... the carrot snatchers! Help! Watch out, Nikki, they're dangerous!"

"Shh!" soothed Nikki. "They are fine... they are my children... they won't hurt you."

"Oh, well!" huffed Herbie, a bit embarrassed by his overreaction, "A rabbit can't be too sure these days!"

Sherlock guided the conversation, "Herbie, say hello and let's get on with today's business."

Herbie looked at the children and decided that any friends of Nikki, Sherlock, and Morph were okay. He held out his paw and said, "Pleased to meet you."

The children giggled at the strange nervous animal and gently shook hands with him, making sure to stay a safe distance from the bucket of carrots.

Asa asked, "So Herbie, if you don't mind my asking, how did you get your name? Or I guess I should say, how did our imaginations come up with it? The meaning must be related somehow to our schoolwork... I got that message already."

Sherlock eagerly interrupted, excited to take on the role of teacher once again. "Quite right! Think about animal science... rabbits and what they eat, including carrots."

Asa jumped in before Prentiss could blurt out the answer, "I've got it! Rabbits eat plants...green stuff and the things you put in salad... no meat... so they are herbivores. Herbie Vore. Hah!"

Sherlock shook his bushy gray tail, "Excellent!! If Herbie did eat plants and animals like humans, his name would have been Omni Vore. Or if he were strictly a meat-eater, you probably would have called him Carni Vore. Herbie is such a lovely name! Thank goodness you stick to plants, my friend."

Herbie thumped his hind leg and replied, "Well, Herbie does suit me just fine! Oh, my, my, my. Asa and Prentiss, let me explain about the carrots. You see..."

"Hold on a bit, Herbie," Sherlock commanded. "That's not how things work with these two young detectives. They discover things in Serendipity by solving clues. Where is Morph? Oh, there she is, flying in circles above the letter box. In all the commotion I lost sight of her."

Turning to Asa and Prentiss, Sherlock continued, "Children, I think some new clues await you. Why don't you go check out the letter box and birdhouse?"

The twins divided up the tasks, Prentiss searching in the mailbox and Asa looking in the birdhouse for a new acorn message. They met their friends back at the gate. Prentiss opened her carefully folded silky message first. She read:

Tea Acoreten

"Oh, brother! Another mixed up word or one I never heard of. How about you, Ace. Have you ever heard of a tea called acoreten?" asked Prentiss.

"Nope! But you know that my clue will have something to do with yours. Let's see what Sherlock has left us!" replied Asa. Sherlock and Nikki laughed as the twins worried over their assignments for today. Herbie continued protecting his carrots. Asa carefully removed the leaf clue from the acorn and read the words aloud:

Two words scrambled but kept apart,
The first is simple so that's where to start,
What seems like tea maybe another word,
Put the first letter last and it won't seem absurd.
As for the second, Science you must use,
Think of carrots and don't blow a fuse,
They have a substance that gives them their hue,
It also helps keep away blindness from people like you.
The letters have been arranged two by two,
Straighten them out and you will have the clue.
Herbie's prize, once you solve it, will brighten your way,
You'll have new vision to help you this day.

Asa jumped up and down with excitement. "This is getting easier or I'm thinking better! The first word isn't tea, but if you put the first letter last you get 'eat.' Eat something."

"That was the easy part, Ace. Now for the second word," Prentiss said seriously as she thought about the second part of the clue. "We know it has something to do with Science and carrots. Carrots are orange, even though they used to be purple and white and all kinds of colors."

"Okay, okay, Pren. Stop with the Science lesson," begged Asa.

"Well, anyway," continued Prentiss, ignoring her brother, "this word is scrambled two letters at a time – two by two. So if we switch around each set, we have carotene – and the orange color in carrots comes from carotene. Eat Carotene." Turning to Sherlock, Prentiss asked, "Do you want us to eat the c-a-r-r-o-t-s?" She was afraid to say the words aloud for fear of throwing Herbie into another tantrum.

Asa jumped into the conversation before Herbie realized what was being suggested. "Yes, if we eat the you-know-whats, we are going to have a new vision, right, Sherlock?"

Nikki beamed with pride at her two humans. "Not so much a new vision, darlings. You will see in your imaginative minds what the future holds for anyone or anything you look at. Like visionaries!"

"That is so cool!" squealed Asa. "But just how do you think we can get some of that prize without making someone around here go haywire?"

Sherlock answered, "Just leave that to us." Turning to Herbie, the squirrel continued, "Herbie, my friend. The twins need your expert advice. They are going to take a journey into the tree groves today. Now you know it gets quite dark in there, right? And since you are an expert at great vision, I think you might be able to assist them. Do you think they might eat just a couple of your carrots so that they can see things more clearly? They won't eat the whole lot! What do you say, chap?"

Herbie was honored to hold such an important role in this day's adventures. He twittered, "Why, when you put it that way, I'd be honored to help." The rabbit chose two of his finest carrots and handed them graciously to Asa and Prentiss. "Please, eat… it is my privilege to serve you."

The twins thanked their new friend and munched on the carrots. They were crisp, juicy, and sweet. After they finished munching, Asa said, "What should we be feeling, Sherlock? I don't feel any different."

"Neither do I," added Prentiss.

"Well, if you think I gave you dud carrots, you are mistaken," grumbled Herbie thumping his hind leg with annoyance.

As usual, Nikki chimed in to keep the peace. "Now, now… the carrots were magnificent, Herbie. And they will work, children, when the time comes. You have received three wonderful gifts so far in Serendipity. Think of a way to use them all to travel on a wonderful adventure that begins over there, through the grove of trees. Now that you are becoming expert detectives, that is all the help we are going to give you. But remember, I will always protect you. Morph will always be above you, your guardian angel. And Sherlock would never ask you to do something that was too difficult for you to achieve. Why, even Herbie won't let you down. You are surrounded by friends and you will grow with the experience. The world is …"

"Our classroom," Prentiss and Asa said in unison. The twins looked at each other and shared the knowledge that whatever new adventures awaited them, they would experience them

together. They took great comfort in knowing that they would always have each other. Asa and Prentiss were also grateful for their friends, old and new, in Serendipity.

"Well, let's get started, Pren. First, why don't you wish us a nice means of transportation. Prentiss nodded and clutched the locket she wore around her neck. Grasping the ray that clicked open she thought of something that she hoped would give Asa a good laugh. Prentiss blinked her eyes and before them stood two faintly familiar items: one gray and one white rocking horse that Papa and Grammy had given the twins in honor of their births. The plush toys each had caramel-colored English bridles and saddles. One stood at the end of each crib in the nursery where Asa and Prentiss spent their first few years. Every night, before they went to bed, the twins galloped atop their horses giggling and babbling with excitement.

The toys were way too small for the twins to ride now and besides, they couldn't really take them very far; that is, without the help of Asa's purple ball. Without saying a word, Asa removed the orb, placed it over the rocking horses, and made his wish. Presto! Not only had the toys become life-sized horses, but they also seemed to be able to move like real equines. The twins laughed at the humorous sight they would create, two eight-year-olds galloping along on toy horses the size of real animals. Asa and Prentiss shrugged their shoulders, a gesture indicating that they realized the ridiculous spectacle they had created, jumped on their steeds, waved good-bye to their friends, and took off in the direction of the groves.

Nikki, in her natural state of worry regarding the children, sighed, "They will be okay. They must be. I hope they don't misuse the carrots. We didn't give them much explanation about their powers."

Sherlock reassured her, "Nikki, we will always be with them. Of course they will be fine. But some things must be attempted independently, right? Now, let's start tracking them. I'm sure your nose is still excellent for a good hunt!"

Nikki barked in agreement and the two were off down the road far enough behind Prentiss and Asa as to not be seen. Morph was already circling above the twins' heads, keeping high enough to remain out of their eyesight. As for Herbie, he scampered around in circles for a few minutes, worrying about where to keep his carrots safely hidden until he returned. Once satisfied, he hopped along the path in leaps and bounds, until he caught up with Sherlock and Nikki.

Asa and Prentiss slowed down their horses as they neared the entrance to the grove. Somehow, the trees appeared much larger and denser than they had from the cottage. Asa led the way into the grove, reminding Prentiss that they had eaten the magic carrots. "Pren, I'm still not sure exactly what being visionaries means. Do you?"

A little frightened by the strange surroundings, Prentiss answered in a hoarse whisper, "No, Ace, I don't. But I'm sure that before this day is through we will find out. Anyway, don't forget that we have the orb and the locket with us. We can always wish our way out of here."

At that moment, one of the large trees right in front of the twins seemed to take on human features. The large trunk and sprawling roots looked like two gnarled feet and legs. The branches took the form of arms with giant, spindly fingers. Two knotholes in the trunk seemed to turn into piercing eyes. The branches at the top looked like an emerald crown. And a larger hole, perhaps once the home of a squirrel, became a gaping mouth. As if awoken from a long nap, the tree grumbled at the twins: "Who gave you permission to enter this grove? Where are your papers?

Do you know the secret password? What's wrong with you two? Does a cat have your tongues? Answer me at once!"

"Who gave you permission to enter this grove? Where are your papers?

Asa and Prentiss trembled with fear. Prentiss spoke first, "Sorry, sir, we didn't mean to trespass. We were sent here by Sherlock, Morph, Herbie, and Nikki. Do you know them?"

"Know them?" roared the tree. "Do you take me for a fool? Of course I know them. But do you know the password? If not, I will turn your silly-looking horses into firewood and you into a nice snack for me!"

"That's silly," whispered Asa to his sister, "Trees are not omnivores or carnivores."

"What was that, you insolent child!" roared the tree. "You have exactly thirty seconds to tell me the password, starting now. Can you read minds? I'll make it easy for you. I'm thinking of the word now."

Asa smiled at his sister. They both concentrated on the giant tree's thoughts. After eating the magic carrots, they could read minds and see the future. They saw in a flash that this tree would not harm them. They also saw the password in the tree's mind, just as if it were painted on a canvas – conifer.

Prentiss shouted, "Conifer, your majesty. That is the password."

"Correct!" roared the tree. "Part two – what is a conifer?"

Asa started to complain about another school problem but changed his mind. Again the twins read the tree's mind. "Trees that have cones, sir," shouted Asa triumphantly.

"Right again. Well, then, young ones, go on with you. Enjoy your stay in the grove. At the end you will find something well worth the journey." With that the tree yawned and turned back into a stationary object.

Asa and Prentiss were proud of the way they handled their first adversary in the grove. They wondered what else would happen to them, but they didn't have very long to wait. When they were about fifty feet from the tree, the horses were spooked by a very strange-looking creature. It had yellow eyes the size of spaceships, slimy green frog's feet, and the most beautiful crimson feathers the twins had ever seen. It surprised the children by swooping down over their heads.

"Hey!" shouted Prentiss, "You frightened our horses."

"Hay is for horses, little fool. And I am not a horse. I am a frowdinal. What are you doing in the grove?"

"Hay is for horses, little fool. And I am not a horse. I am a frowdinal. What are you doing in the grove?"

"Excuse me for asking, but what exactly is a frowdinal?" Prentiss said bravely.

"A frowdinal is a fine animal with the beautiful eyes of an owl, the sturdy feet of a frog, and the absolutely gorgeous feathers of a cardinal. Red is my color, don't you agree?"

Trying to start off on better terms than with the tree, Prentiss replied, "Oh, yes. Red is definitely lovely on you."

"Thank you. You see, I am the last of my kind. I got left behind when the flock took off for other lands. I was trying to help Herbie find where he left his carrots and off they went. Now I don't know how to find them and I'm afraid the magic carrots don't work on me. I am stuck here in this grove forever. Now, who are you? Nice feathers atop your heads, but you must be cold with all that skin showing everywhere else. Were you plucked by some evil demon? What kind of creatures are you?"

The children tried to hold back their giggles. "Why, we're humans. My name is Asa and this is my sister, Prentiss."

"Humans, did you say? I don't suppose you've eaten any magic carrots lately? Herbie said they work just fine on mammals and humans are mammals, right?"

Prentiss replied, "Yes, ma'am, we have eaten the carrots. Herbie is our newest friend in Serendipity. We will help you if you wish. It must be terrible to be left behind."

The frowdinal seemed pleased. She told the twins to concentrate on the furthest tree in the grove and see if they could figure out where the flock headed after it passed this point. The vision came quickly. The flock had headed south. A map appeared in their minds and the twins gave the frowdinal the information she needed. The creature told Asa and Prentiss to look in the nest above the branch where she was perched. The frowdinal said goodbye to her human friends and flew off to join the flock. Prentiss asked her brother, "Do you think she'll make it, Ace?"

"I'm sure of it. My vision showed her in the future, flying with her family. So, let's check out the nest and head home. I'm done with this crazy grove."

The twins worked together. Prentiss climbed on Asa's shoulders and carefully looked inside the nest. There she found a beautiful ruby-studded feather quill. The feather matched the lovely cardinal ones of the frowdinal. Just as she was about to pick up the pen, it floated into the air and wrote these words, just like a sky writer plane:

"My gift to you is this pen. It can only write the truth. Take care of it and think of me always. If you ever need me, I will be at your side in your wonderful imaginations."

"Well, Pren, it's your turn to be keeper of the gift. Keep the pen safe. We may need it sometime." Just as Asa was finishing his sentence, he heard familiar voices.

"Asa, Prentiss, we're right here! How are you?" shouted Nikki.

"Nikki, over here," answered Asa. "We're fine. Lots of adventures! Fun, too. How did you get here so fast? Oh, never mind! I forgot for a minute that I was in Serendipity where anything could happen. Well, we're glad to see you!"

Prentiss chimed in, "Oh, Nikki, Sherlock, and Morph! Oh, hi, Herbie. Your carrots are wonderful. They saved our skins and helped the frowdinal get home. And oh this has been so much fun." Prentiss was talking a mile a minute.

"Slow down, girl, you'll break something!" teased Sherlock.

"Oh, dear, my carrots, my carrots! Now where did I leave them? Oh, not again, not again. What shall I do?" cried Herbie in a frenzy.

Asa peered into Herbie's mind and answered, "Herbie, your carrots are safe. You left them inside our cottage on the table near the orange door and blue rug. I can see them clearly in your mind."

"Thank you, boy," said Herbie a little less rattled. "Yes, yes I remember. The cottage, yes inside. Well come along… Let's all go home. I will make a carrot stew. Lovely day isn't it?"

Prentiss and Asa mounted their horses and took off for the magic cottage. Morph, Sherlock, and Nikki followed closely behind. Herbie managed to keep up after a few false starts when he thumped around in circles. Morph circled effortlessly above the children's heads. The troop of friends was growing each day along with many wonderful adventures that the twins relished. By the time they got back to the cottage, turned the horses back into toys, helped Herbie get his carrots, and said good-bye to their friends, it was time once again to leave Serendipity for the cozy haven of Papa and Grammy's house.

They arrived at their grandparents' house and immediately picked up the sweet aroma of carrots simmering in a large cast iron pot on the stove. Grammy turned to her grandchildren, hugged them and said, "Hello, sweet peas! Care for some carrot stew?"

Asa chuckled and said, "I've had my fill of carrots for today, thank you." Prentiss pinched her brother hard enough to leave a mark on his upper arm. Asa turned to retaliate when he caught the look in his twin's eyes. He had almost spilled the beans about the magic carrots. He saved the situation by adding, "Of course, the other carrots were just pretend magic carrots, and your carrot stew smells so wonderful, Grammy, I know there is always room for more…er… I mean for real carrots!"

After a wonderful supper, Asa and Prentiss dragged their tired bodies up to bed. As they pulled back the soft comforters Prentiss said, "Asa, isn't that strange that Grammy cooked carrots today? And did you see her wink at Papa again when you opened your big mouth about Herbie's carrots? There are so many weird things going on around here – strange and wonderful. I've never had so much fun! Do you think we'll ever see the frowdinal again? And Herbie… isn't he darling? Kind of nervous and jittery but so cute!"

Asa was too exhausted to answer. He yawned and managed to say, "Save it, Pren. Tomorrow… is another…"

Prentiss finished the thought in her brother's mind. They both wondered what could possibly happen next. They only had to wait to sleep through a night of beautiful dreams to discover the answer to that question.

Chapter Five
Acapella

Prentiss and Asa awoke to the aromas of French toast, bacon and eggs and the sounds of Grammy's soprano voice singing familiar tunes from one of the musicals. They knew that Papa was in the kitchen cooking. He was a gourmet chef and loved to surprise his grandchildren with new recipes. They would find breakfast waiting for them on the large kitchen table, the food artistically placed on each plate: The French toast in the shape of a lion or tiger, the bacon forming swords atop two perfectly cooked eggs. Grammy was in rare form this morning, singing one of her favorite songs that had something to do with memories. As the twins greeted their grandparents in the kitchen, they joined in with Grammy, forming an a capella choir – no instruments besides the lovely voices of eight-year-old children and their melodic grandmother:

Memories are for keeping
Dreams are for sleeping
Make believe is for teaching
The future you might be reaching.
Never stop believing
Each thought is worth retrieving.
The magic lies within your heart
That's where our love will never part.

When Grammy heard the children's angelic voices, she hugged each of them and said, "You sing like little cherubs. I am so glad your mommy kept our family tradition of singing the musicals to you. I remember when you were just babes... not even walking yet. Every night you had music time with your mom and dad. Asa, you especially would jump up and down with glee, your little body bouncing to the rhythm. Music is a gift... it warms the heart and sends powerful energy to the mind. Well, enough of that. I am sure you two are ready for the hearty breakfast Papa made especially for you. And, you must be ready for your day's adventures."

"We love to sing with you, Grammy," Asa said as he gave his Grammy a huge bear hug. The boy had a knack for hugging people just the right way. "And we still have music time at home with Mommy and Daddy. We are the only kids in our class who know all the words to the musicals. Most of them don't even know the tunes!"

"I love that song, Grammy," added Prentiss. "The part about make believe reminds me of something."

Asa gave his sister a quick look. He was afraid she would tell Papa and Grammy all about Serendipity and that somehow their magical world would disappear. Prentiss got the hint and changed the subject: "I'm starving, Papa. Boy, the French toast giraffes look too good to eat! You are an artist!!"

"Thank you, Asa. We are a family of musicians and artists. Each one of us has special gifts. You two are young, but you will discover your talents. Be patient. So you like the giraffes, eh? Anything for my sweethearts," chuckled Papa. "Go ahead and eat!"

The twins tried not to gulp down their food, but they were anxious to return to Serendipity. Soon they were off with their packed lunches in hand and all their special gifts they had received in their magic land.

Asa and Prentiss had an uneventful ride in the transporter and eagerly ran to the magic cottage. Nikki was rocking in the red chair, as usual, with Sherlock perched on her head. Morph was flitting around the flowers in the planter. Herbie was scampering all over the yard. He had misplaced the red bucket filled with his magic carrots. Asa and Prentiss greeted their friends and

assisted Herbie in finding his bucket. As soon as this task was accomplished, Asa ran to the birdhouse and Prentiss skipped over to the mailbox.

Sherlock said, "My, my, my... two children are in a very big hurry to discover new clues today. Well, go on! Let's see what you find!"

Prentiss unfolded the silky paper that she found inside the mailbox and read aloud:

A cape all

Asa carefully stuck his hand inside the birdhouse and pulled out a very small acorn. He immediately saw the tooth-marked hole on one end. The boy carefully pulled out the leaf message and said:

Adventures can happen outside and within,
This one in Asa's bedroom will begin,
What once was missing will now appear,
Beautiful music you shall hear.
The voice is an instrument sturdy and bright,
It carries sweet notes right into the light.
A new friend appears, she will take you far,
Up to the clouds and past every star,
If you sing her name she will make herself seen,
A voice with no other instruments, that's what her name
means.

"Ace," Prentiss squealed. "This one is easy. Why, Grammy gave us some clues today. Almost as if she knew what we would find... but that's impossible, isn't it?"

"Pren," Asa added, "Nothing is impossible in Serendipity. I get the clues, too. My bedroom, new friend, sing her name."

"Yes," added Prentiss, "And her name means music with no instruments except the voice. Look at the scrambled word... a cape all... a capella. That must be the name we need to sing."

"What are we waiting for?" asked Asa, already leaping through the front door and through the long hallway into his bedroom.

Prentiss ran right behind her brother. When they reached Asa's bedroom, the twins began singing in perfect harmony, "a capella, a capella."

They heard a commotion up in Asa's loft and quickly made their way up the ladder. The marigold light brightened the room. There, before the siblings' eyes stood a golden birdcage. Inside, a beautiful red-feathered bird was perched on a stand. Both children immediately thought of the frowdinal they had met yesterday in the groves. This bird had the same red feathers, but did not have the big owl eyes or slimy green frog's feet. In fact, the new addition to Serendipity was a perfectly beautiful specimen of a cardinal.

What shocked Asa and Prentiss most was that the cardinal was singing the same tune that they had heard this morning, Grammy's Memories song.

Memories are for keeping
Dreams are for sleeping
Make believe is for teaching
The future you might be reaching.
Never stop believing
Each thought is worth retrieving.
The magic lies within your heart
That's where our love will never part.

The twins joined right in with Acapella's performance which encouraged the bird to sing louder. When they finished the tune, Herbie, Sherlock, and Nikki applauded each in their own way: the rabbit thumping his hind leg, the squirrel pounding his bushy tail against the wall, and the dog jumping up and down on softly padded feet. Morph effortlessly managed perfect circles in the air to express her delight.

The children bowed graciously to their audience and the bird ruffled her feathers. "Thank you so much," added Prentiss graciously. Turning to the bird she said, "I presume you are Acapella."

"Correct, my dear," replied the cardinal. "And I presume you are Prentiss and Asa. I am so glad to meet you. I have heard wonderful things about you."

"You have a beautiful voice," commented Asa. "May I ask why you are all caged up? I mean, it's a beautiful gold cage, but why aren't you free like everything else in Serendipity?"

The bird rustled her feathers to fluff them up and answered, "Young humans, the cage does not keep me in. I can come and go as I please. But it does allow me to keep enemies out. It is a safe place for me. You will find in life that freedom is mostly how you think about things. Some creatures are trapped by bad thoughts or an unimaginative mind. They stop using the imagination muscle and it becomes stiff. Eventually it just withers away. These beings lose their independence. They are dependent on others for their happiness, their way of life, what they should like and what they should dislike. They are the saddest living things. But those individuals who keep the imagination perfectly tuned, sing their way through life. They may travel anywhere they choose, physically or mentally. They possess certain gifts that help them discover something new everyday. Do you understand?"

Asa answered first. "I think so. I think I am beginning to understand why we have received each of our gifts – they have been in our minds all the time. We just needed help in understanding how to use them and how to exercise our imaginations. That is so cool. So please tell me, Acapella, does that mean today is going to be a music day?" Asa hoped the answer would be yes. He loved music more than anything else.

"Correct, Asa," replied the bird. "Today we reach the clouds and enjoy a concert like none you have ever heard before. So, are you ready? Not quite, I think. Prentiss, you hold the golden locket. I think you and your brother are going to need some umbrellas."

With a nod of her head, Prentiss held the locket that still hung around her neck and performed the actions necessary to make the gift work. Two umbrellas quickly appeared at her feet.

"Good job, miss," chirped the cardinal. "Now, Asa, I want you to carefully place the purple orb above my head. Right now, I am too small for the two of you to ride. But with your powers, Asa, you can enlarge me. Don't be afraid, you won't hurt me."

Asa looked for support from Nikki and Sherlock, who both nodded their approval and reassurance. Carefully, Asa removed the tiny purple ball from his pocket and placed it above the head of the gorgeous scarlet bird. Immediately, she grew in size and had to flutter outside the shuttered window, for she had grown too big for her cage or the bedroom.

"Now, before we go, make sure you also have your other gifts. Herbie, please provide our young explorers with some of your magic carrots. They may be useful during our adventure. Prentiss, make sure you have the magic feather quill. Can you manage everything… the pen, your locket, and the umbrellas?"

Prentiss proudly remarked, "Yes, I can, Acapella. I promise to keep everything safe. Cross my heart!"

After the children consumed the magic carrots and packed their items, they climbed on Acapella's back. Asa had one more question: "Is it rude to ask just where we are going?"

"Not rude," answered Acapella. "But I would rather you be surprised. Besides, you have the clues from this morning. You will soon see for yourself."

Asa remembered the poem he had pulled from the acorn. "So I take it we are going to fly up into the sky and go somewhere far away from here."

But without answering, Acapella flew off, giving the children just seconds to turn and wave goodbye to their Serendipity friends. Nikki nervously yelped with motherly concern for her children. Sherlock hopped onto her head, reassuring the dog that all would be well. Morph flew behind Acapella and Herbie went into the garden to tend to his carrots.

Asa and Prentiss enjoyed the ride provided by the strong wings of Acapella. They soared high above the trees.

Asa and Prentiss enjoyed the ride provided by the strong wings of Acapella. They soared high above the trees. The Sunflower Queen shone so brightly that the children had to wince to see. The trip did not take long. Before they knew it, Acapella slowed down and landed inside one of the many cotton-ball clouds the children had admired when they first arrived in Serendipity. They had no idea that whole kingdoms existed inside the clouds. Acapella returned to her normal bird size and told the twins to open their umbrellas.

"Why do we need umbrellas?" Prentiss asked.

"Well, all the residents of this cloud are birds of one kind or another. They are a happy group, always singing. But, they are birds and birds tend to, well, have little accidents when they get happy. The umbrellas are to protect your heads and clothing from...er....these little mistakes. Well, it is just the wonder of nature, you know. It can't be helped."

Asa nudged his sister. "I get it! Bird poop! They're poop umbrellas!"

Prentiss nudged her brother back and told him to be quiet and watch his manners. She wondered why boys were so disgusting! They gulped their food, constantly burped, and said nasty things. Girls were so much more polite. She hoped Asa would not do something gross. After all, they were guests in this strange place.

Soon the threesome marched off toward an incredibly beautiful ivory white castle that sat at the far end of the cloud. The structure had magnificent towers, a golden drawbridge, and sparkling white doves adorning each window. The visitors made their way across the bridge. As soon as they entered the castle, their ears were greeted by the most beautiful music the twins had ever heard. They couldn't keep their bodies from swaying to the melodies. Asa began dancing around, as if he were alone in this magical kingdom, swept up by the magical sounds. Prentiss enjoyed watching her talented brother move as much as she enjoyed the music. She thought to herself, "This day is for you, little brother. Have fun with the music. Dance. I'm glad I'm here to see this beautiful place and hear the music. And maybe, another day will be my special time in Serendipity!"

Every bird from the bird kingdom was present, each with its own unique voice. Each one swooped carefully down to greet the children and make introductions. One in particular made the children freeze with astonishment. It was a lovely little bird, no bigger than Papa's hand. Its silky soft feathers were the color of ripe green apples, a love bird. Asa remembered that their mother had owned one when she was a child. A tragedy occurred once that made Grammy sad to this day. The bird loved to ride around the house on top of people's heads. One day he perched himself on top of Grammy's head. The doorbell rang and Grammy forgot that the bird was stationed above. When the door opened, the love bird flew away, never to return. Mommy was crushed and Grammy was heartsick. But time passed and the pain healed.

Prentiss punched her brother's arm to bring him back to the present: "Ace, this love bird is trying to introduce himself. Pay attention."

Asa came to and gave his full attention to the bird, "How do you do. My name is Asa."

"I know who you are, young human. And I am Johann Sebastian Bird."

Asa and Prentiss stared at each other in disbelief. Prentiss now remembered the name of the lost bird, too. His name was Johann Sebastian, but his nickname was Sebastian. Could it be true? Prentiss wished she had a camera so that she could take a picture of the lost friend to show Mommy. At the time she made the wish, she was clutching the golden locket. Poof!

A digital camera appeared at her feet. The young girl shuddered for a moment, worried that Grammy and Papa would not approve of the electronic device – no electronics, no computers, no anything but our imaginations.

In the meantime, Asa asked the bird: "Are you our mom's Sebastian? The very one?"

"Are you our mom's Sebastian? The very one?"

"Well, of course I am. And as you can see, I am just fine. Please send my regards to your mother and grandparents. Tell your Grammy that I had planned this voyage for a long time. It was not her fault. She just made it possible for me to go. Parting from our loved ones is always a sad affair. Thank goodness for fond memories. I loved your mother dearly, but I had to test my musical abilities up here in Serendipity. Sometimes we have to take chances, you know. They make life very interesting." Turning to Prentiss he added, "Prentiss, the camera may look like a regular one, but you should know by now that nothing is what it seems in this world. Would you like to take a group picture?"

The twins nodded. Acapella took the camera in her beak so that Prentiss and Asa could take a photo with Sebastian. They all posed nicely. When the camera was supposed to click, something strange happened. The magic feather quill floated out of Prentice's pocket. In the air, it painted a beautiful portrait of the bird and children. When it was complete, the painting floated into the lens of the camera, ready to be developed at a later date. Prentiss laughed, "I should've known!"

The quill floated back into Prentiss's pocket and she put the camera away for safekeeping. Holding their umbrellas, the twins followed Sebastian and Acapella into the largest auditorium they had ever seen. Thousands of birds were inside, some flying above and some on stage. The musical performances sounded like angels singing in heaven. The twins were glad that they had their umbrellas. Nature was taking its course for the flying birds above their heads.

The avian choir sang songs from every musical the children had ever heard. Asa became so entranced that he hypnotically joined the birds on the stage, singing and dancing as lovely as any star performer. He was naturally in tune with the music. His sturdy, boyish legs moved gracefully yet powerfully. Watching her twin, Prentiss wondered if Asa would be a famous dancer someday. She liked music, too, but he seemed crazy about it; as if it hypnotized him. After what seemed like hours, Acapella warned the twins that they would have to return to the cottage.

Sebastian came to say good-bye. "I have a gift for you, which should come as no surprise. By now you know that each new friend that you meet in Serendipity will provide you with something to help you use your imaginations to their fullest powers. My gift is simple. Please accept one of my green feathers. It is not just any plume, but one that will provide you with the music of hope and courage wherever you go. Asa, I believe it is your turn to be the keeper of the gift for you and your sister. Please accept it with my thanks and give your mother a special kiss for me."

As Asa took the feather from Sebastian, he heard a symphony of happiness coming from the plume. At once he felt confident and secure. By the glistening in her eyes, Asa could tell that Prentiss felt the same magic. Sebastian accompanied Acapella and the twins to the drawbridge where they made their final goodbyes. Morph had been waiting there, keeping out of sight. Asa reluctantly pulled out the purple ball and held it over the cardinal's head. She instantly grew in size. The twins climbed aboard and started off towards the magic cottage. Within minutes, Asa and Prentiss were riding comfortably on the back of their new friend. They each held a closed umbrella in one hand and kept the magic gifts they had received in Serendipity safely packed away. Suddenly, the sky became very dark. They heard rumblings close by that they recognized as thunder. A storm was setting in.

"Hang on, children," warned Acapella. "It will become difficult for me to see in a few seconds. This is going to be quite a storm! Too strong for your umbrellas, I'm afraid. You are going to get wet!"

The twins became frightened as they heard the thunder growing louder and the lightening flashes coming closer. They feared that Acapella would not be able to stay airborne through such a terrible storm. Each in his or her own way took inventory of the special Serendipity gifts and tried to think of a quick plan that could lead them to safety.

Asa thought of something quickly. "Prentiss, you and I ate the carrots this morning. Let's use them to focus on the next cloud so that maybe we can make a path for Acapella that will take us safely back to the cottage."

Prentiss wasn't sure this would work, but she couldn't think of anything better. "We have to do something and soon! Acapella can't fly much longer. It seems like we already are losing our place among the clouds. Okay! Let's see if the carrots can help!"

At that very moment, a bolt of lightening came so close to their heads that both children shrieked. Acapella dodged the bolt by swooping below it. The children squeezed their eyes shut to focus on the lowest cloud they could see. They saw a path through the storm, lit by a familiar yellow glow. The Sunflower Queen appeared in their vision, as if she swept the threatening clouds apart like stage curtains. Suddenly, a beautiful rainbow formed, leading from this cloud right down to Asa's loft window. As the party flew down the path to safety, Asa and Prentiss looked back to see where they had been. Both children wondered at the image in their minds: The Sunflower Queen using her hand-like rays to smooth out the rainbow like a fine carpet, to calm the storm, and to embrace the children in a blanket of warmth.

Acapella was able to transport the children and herself safely back to the cottage. Fortunately, children and birds don't melt in the midst of storms. They all dried off and eagerly shared their adventures with Herbie, Nikki, and Sherlock. The twins noticed that Morph was nowhere to be seen. They called her name. The tiny butterfly climbed out from under one of the closed umbrellas. When they returned from the concert and stood at the drawbridge, Morph hid under one of the umbrellas, an action that proved wise with the coming of the storm. Everyone was glad to see that Morph was safe, their guardian angel who risked her life to assure the children returned without any harm done to them. The children stared up through the half-moon window to catch a glimpse of another heroine, The Sunflower Queen. She seemed to be smiling down at them.

Prentiss and Asa knew that it was time for them to take the last leg of their trip for the day back to Papa and Grammy's house using their transporter. They were tired but filled with joy, the music from the concert lingering in their young ears. They knew that they carried new memories with them that would fill their parents and grandparents' hearts with joy… an old friend found… Johann Sebastian Bird… and new ones who added the gift of music to their imaginations.

The children said goodbye once again to their friends. They climbed down the ladder in Asa's loft as Acapella settled in for an afternoon nap on the perch inside her golden cage. As they were leaving Asa's bedroom, Prentiss thought she heard a baby crying in her bedroom. She asked, "What was that?"

Apparently no one else had heard the sound. Too tired to investigate now, Prentiss was determined to check out the noise tomorrow. Right now she hungered for the soft quilts and fluffy pillow that waited for her on her bed at her grandparents' house.

Asa was content with the images dancing in his head. He thought to himself, "Music is my life. It always will be a part of whatever I do." With that thought he arrived safely at his grandparents' front door, his sister next to him. Both children were too tired to speak, even to each other. They both had wonderful dreams that swept them back to their adventures in Serendipity, neither realizing that many new experiences were awaiting them.

Chapter Six
Rembrandt

"Pren, hold up! Why are you in such a hurry to get to the cottage?" shouted Asa trailing behind his sister as the twins landed in Serendipity. "I told you before, Ace. I heard a noise coming from my bedroom yesterday. I'm going to find out what it was."

Asa knew better than to argue with his sister when she had that stubborn tone in her voice. Nothing would stop her from completing her task, no matter what it took. Prentiss would not give up, and Asa saw this as a gift instead of a curse. He imagined his sister as a famous inventor someday, unwilling to call it quits because the first thousand or so experiments failed. Not Prentiss. So Asa chose to follow his sister into the magic cottage and up to the top of her loft. On the way he peeked into his room and noticed that Acapella was sleeping soundly in her cage. He hoped that he would have time to sing with her again. Asa started humming a song.

"Ace, shh! I don't want to scare anything that might be in my room!" commanded Prentiss.

The twins listened quietly. At first they couldn't hear or see anything unusual. Moments later they heard a thud from the shuttered window that framed the front wall of the bedroom. There on the window sill lazed a beautiful white cat, the color of undisturbed snow; although, she wasn't completely white. It was as if someone had held her by the tip of the tail and dipped her into white paint, for the tail tip was as black as ebony.

**There on the window sill lazed a beautiful white cat, the
color of undisturbed snow; although, she wasn't completely
white. It was as if someone had held her by the tip of the
tail and dipped her into white paint, for the tail tip was as
black as ebony.**

Prentiss tiptoed up to the feline to see if she could get a better look. "Meooowww!" screeched the cat as she arched her back. Prentiss realized that that was the sound she had heard yesterday. Cat's meows often sounded like babies crying, she recalled. The child stepped back and muttered, "So sorry to bother you! But this is my room. How do you do? I'm Prentiss."

The cat now recovered from her fright and said in perfect English, "Yes, child, I know who you both are. I am quite good friends with Nikki, Sherlock, Herbie, Morph, and Acapella. I hear you had quite an adventure yesterday. Sorry I missed it but I was painting a mural on the far side of the hill. I thought I would wear out my tail with all the work I had to do. You see, my lovely tail makes a perfect paintbrush. I finished just before that awful storm hit. By the way, my name is Rembrandt."

Prentiss smiled, "Rembrandt? Like the painter?"

Rembrandt corrected, "Like the artist, child, like the artist. Yes, you might say we share the same talent as well as the same name. Do you like to paint?"

Prentiss almost burst with excitement. "Do I like to paint? I love it! There's no better way to tell a story. I love to imagine new places and create new creatures. I don't like following other people's ideas. I simply hate paint by numbers and coloring books. I can't use my own ideas. I like just plain paper and my paints. Then I wait for the visions to come and there you have it!"

"Clever girl!" commented the cat. "What about you, Asa? Do you like art."

"Yes, of course," answered the young boy. "But not as much as my sister. She's as wild about art as I am about music."

"I just wish I were better at painting," pouted Prentiss. "Sometimes I can't get the picture to look like the idea in my head. I get so angry!"

"Boy, you can say that again! When Pren gets angry watch out! Things start flying!" laughed Asa.

"Well, painting is an art that takes practice. The other Rembrandt once said, *'Practice what you know, and it will help to make clear what now you do not know.'* " The cat licked her paw and used it as a brush to comb her silky white fur.

"Rembrandt, do you think you might show me... I mean us... your mural? I would love to see your art," begged Prentiss.

"I think that might be arranged. The more experiences you have, the more you will learn about the world. Your art will become perfected by what you feel inside your heart and soul."

Prentiss was instantly becoming a fan of the four-legged artist. Asa was interested in what new adventures the twins were about to experience.

"So, where's this mural?" asked Asa, trying to move the group outdoors again.

"Follow me. I'll show you," replied Rembrandt.

Once the trio got into the living area, they were greeted by Nikki, Herbie, Sherlock, Morph, and Acapella who had awakened from her nap and joined the others. Greetings were given all around and Nikki licked the round faces of her humans.

Sherlock asked, "Just where are the three of you headed this fine morning? Are you so busy that you forgot, Asa and Prentiss, to check the birdhouse and letter box for messages?"

"We're so sorry, Sherlock," apologized Prentiss. "It's my fault. I got so excited about meeting Rembrandt and seeing her art that I'm afraid I forgot completely about our jobs as detectives in Serendipity. Come on, Ace, let's go check things out now!" With that Prentiss bolted out the door. Asa ran to the birdhouse as usual and Prentiss took the mailbox. Both sites were completely empty.

"Why are there no messages?" asked Asa. "Did we fail?"

Sherlock laughed and replied, "No, no, Asa. All is well. Things will be a bit different today, right! Don't forget, you do have the other gifts already. Use them to figure out your problem for today."

The children looked confused but pulled out their most valued treasures. Prentiss could not think of anything to wish for with her golden locket or the feather quill. Likewise, Asa could not come up with a practical use for the purple ball or the green feather. Not yet, anyway. The twins also had the magnifying glass and the camera that painted pictures. They thought a few magic carrots couldn't hurt, so they asked Herbie for some of his stew. The rabbit graciously gave each twin a heaping portion of his concoction. They stared at Rembrandt, hoping that they could envision what it is they needed to know. Both twins received a mental image of the largest mural they had ever seen, complete with every color of the rainbow. They knew this mural had something to do with their future adventure, but they still did not have any idea how to begin. But when Asa took the green feather out of his pocket and when Prentiss removed the red feather quill from hers, something miraculous happened. The feather began playing a beautiful song, like none the children had ever heard. The crimson quill danced to the music and wrote the following:

The world is your palette, your minds hold the key,
Sweet music will keep you in perfect harmony.
Go back to the stone that held the first clue,
Look again in this spot to see what's in store for you,
What you thought held no secrets, were hidden you see,
Look right at the mailbox to solve this mystery.
Keep your imaginations open and don't hesitate,
Find the artists inside you before it's too late.

Prentiss and Asa used their special bonding to read each other's thoughts. They both ran to the black stone in the pathway near the gate, the very place where the twins discovered the golden locket. There, right in front of them in plain view, they saw two artists' berets, as black as the stone itself. In fact, the hats had blended right into the stone. They quickly picked up the berets and placed them on their heads. As soon as they did, tubes of the finest oil paints popped into their hands. Nikki wagged her tail with approval and Sherlock nodded his head.

Next, Asa and Prentiss ran to the mailbox. Rather than looking inside as they usually did, they examined the exterior of the box. Camouflaged with the same colors as the mailbox, they found two professional paint brushes. The children carefully examined their new gifts. Asa said, "Let me guess! With these brushes we will be able to paint whatever we imagine!!"

"Bravo!" shouted Sherlock.

Morph did somersaults of happiness above the children's heads. Without any prodding from Sherlock, the twins used the visionary powers that they received from the magic carrots. They concentrated on the new gifts and saw that Rembrandt's mural was somehow three dimensional and that they would be visiting this special place quite soon. They both wished for a map to take them to the mural and one appeared, just as Prentiss pressed on the golden locket. The twins realized that their gifts began to add up and that they might need help carrying things to the next adventure. They looked around and discovered a red wagon, just like the one they had at home, standing between the trees next to the cottage.

Asa went to fetch the wagon as Sherlock told the twins, "You see, you are becoming more independent each day. Why we hardly had to give you any coaxing to get ready for this adventure. Today marks a new stage in your imagination education. We will all wait for you at the cottage, except for Rembrandt. You will have to rely on each other and on Rembrandt, of course, to make your way to and from the mural world. But you will be just fine. You are both intelligent beyond your years. You do not give up and you use all your gifts to discover solutions to your problems. We all believe in you.

Believe in yourselves. Now, go with Rembrandt. This is your special day, Prentiss, one filled with the mysteries of art, but you of course will enjoy it also, Asa. Your special twin bonds let you help each other understand this world in ways that others never experience. Go now! Enjoy!"

With that, Sherlock, Morph, Herbie, Acapella, and Nikki went inside the cottage. As she was going through the entrance, Nikki turned to take one last look at her children. Prentiss swore that she saw a tear falling from the dog's eye. In their hearts, both children felt a bit nervous about the unknown adventure before them. They had never felt so alone. But they did have Rembrandt, even though the cat was not exactly warm and friendly like the others. She seemed more absorbed in her own world, often sprinting ahead and then remembering at the last minute that the twins, tugging the wagon laden with art supplies, were behind her. But somehow, after what seemed like hours, the journey ended in a lovely field of wildflowers that fell like a large rainbow-blanket of colors before them.

"Well, we're here!" announced Rembrandt, licking her fur with her long sandpaper tongue. "I do think these wildflowers are the most beautiful I've painted. Do you like my floral mural?"

Prentiss said with awe, "Oh, yes! It's magnificent!"

Rembrandt just kept licking her fur, but Prentiss noticed the cat started purring as the girl gave the compliment.

"Now what?" asked Prentiss.

"Oh, that's right. This is your first time. I do forget these things," said the cat. "Well, first off, straighten the berets on your heads. You are going into the art world of Serendipity. The children obediently straightened the black berets on their heads. Rembrandt continued giving instructions: "Asa, park the wagon, it will be safe here. Take out all the supplies you will need… and that's it! Just follow me!"

Knowing how the cat almost left them several times on their journey thus far, the twins worked quickly completing each task in record time. The next thing that happened made the children a bit fearful, but they followed the leader anyway. Rembrandt leaped right into the middle of her flowerbed mural and disappeared. Asa and Prentiss followed suit. Soon they were nowhere to be seen from the fields of Serendipity.

Once the children took the leap of faith, they found themselves swimming through a sea of oil colors. Everything in this world was created from fresh paint! The remarkable thing was that the pasty liquids did not stick to their bodies or clothes. After what seemed like hours, Rembrandt stopped in front of them and rested on what seemed to be an empty canvas. The strange thing was that the beautiful wildflowers surrounded the cat and the twins like a huge frame.

"Well," said Rembrandt, "I think you can see the large task in front of us. We must finish this piece of the canvas. The problem is, what to paint? Ideas, class?"

Asa was about to remark about being in school again but held his tongue. Prentiss thought for awhile and then blurted out, "Let's make a circus, a big beautiful circus with elephants, tigers, tightrope walkers and trapeze artists! Oh, can we, Rembrandt?"

"Let's make a circus, a big beautiful circus with elephants, tigers, tightrope walkers and trapeze artists.

The cat slowly turned her head toward the young girl, "This is your adventure, Prentiss. If you wish to paint a circus, then a circus it is." Rembrandt stretched out her lean body and yawned. "Well, you two young artists get started. I need a nap."

"But, how? Where? What do I do first?" whined Prentiss.

"Begin with what you know. Begin with what you know" repeated Rembrandt in a sing-song voice.

Asa tried to reassure his sister, "It's okay, Pren. You don't need Rembrandt! She's probably run off somewhere to clean herself or barf up fur balls. Think of the many times Mommy and Daddy have taken us to the circus. Draw what you remember; what's in your heart."

The words of confidence hit home. Soon Prentiss was sketching three rings; a red and white striped canopy overhead; crowds of people sitting excitedly on benches watching the main attractions; colorful clowns riding in tiny cars and exploding bottles in front of the crowds, dowsing the audience with confetti. In the center ring, Prentiss drew trapeze artists swinging bravely above the heads of the audience with no net to catch them below. The right ring held a tiger act, ferocious cats obeying the tamer's commands to sit, roll over each other, and jump through hoops of fire. The left ring vibrated with the steps of giant elephants, forming a circle by holding each other's tails with their massive trunks. Prentiss's canvas was magnificent. Asa noticed that sitting right in the center of the middle group of benches were Grammy, Papa, Mommy, Daddy, and the twins. He wondered if it were possible to be two places at once, but then again, this was Serendipity and anything was possible.

When she was quite satisfied with her creation, Prentiss touched her brother's shoulder and said, "Your turn, Ace. Add the music. Then the picture will be complete. Music and art belong together just like you and me. They are connected with a special bond that can never be broken. Please, Ace. Do it for me."

Asa felt so filled with emotion that he dared not speak for fear he would cry. After all, he was a boy and bigger and stronger than his sister. And boys didn't like to cry in front of girls; even sisters. He took hold of his emotions, removed the green feather from his pocket and thought of all the sounds he could remember from his experiences at the circus. His magic worked. The paint world was filled with the music: tympanic drums, strong horns, and delicate strings. It was magnificent.

"Ace, let's go. Let's jump in to the canvas. I've always wanted to fly on a trapeze. What about you?"

"Why not?"

Holding hands to gain confidence, the twins jumped into the center ring, climbed the never-ending ropes to the top of the trapeze swings and joined the trapeze artists at the top of the world. As the children looked down at the pea-sized audience, they noticed that they no longer were sitting with their family. Their clothes had also transformed into sparkling leotards – Asa's black with gold sparkles and Prentiss's a bright magenta with rose pink sparkles. She also wore a beautiful diamond tiara in her hair.

They heard applause and saw lots of ant-size arms pointing up to the trapeze. The people were looking at them. Prentiss and Asa had become the center of attraction. Not knowing how, the twins began to perform amazing tricks: double and triple somersaults, quadruple twists. They worked in complete harmony, probably from years of being together. Asa and Prentiss had never experienced anything like this before. They felt like birds soaring through the air as their fingers left the safety of the bars and their elastic bodies twirled in perfect harmony. They never doubted for a minute that their partner would fail to catch them, and when the twins' hands clasped each other as a perfect fit, yin and yang, they knew that this adventure proved the power of love to move mountains, to make dreams come true, especially in Serendipity. This was an experience of a lifetime – one that the brother and sister would happily remember for years to come.

After awhile, the circus canvas began to dry. They heard Rembrandt calling them, "Asa, Prentiss, you must leave now. The canvas is done. We must go back to the cottage. By the way, nice work. Your canvas moves with excitement. The animals seem real and the trapeze stars are the focus of the show. Well," she purred, "You did have a remarkable teacher, now didn't you?"

The twins looked at each other and giggled and then turned back to take one last look at their creation. Asa took pride in knowing he had helped, but the true artist was his sister. She had a knack for choosing just the right colors. The painted figures burst with life and seemed to jump right out of the canvas.

Prentiss felt quite proud of herself. She remembered the camera that was in her pocket and decided to take a picture of her circus masterpiece. Once again, the scene was painted onto a canvas and flipped back into the camera. Prentiss was pleased. She knew that she was not always an easy person to be around. When she had an idea, things had to be her way or no way. She looked lovingly at her brother. She saw in Asa a true friend, one who sometimes let her take the star role. But his support was always there. He had a big heart and a kind soul. Although they sometimes fought over silly things like most brothers and sisters, they also truly understood each other, better than anyone else in the world. She would remember this day always as her special adventure shared with her by her new friend, Rembrandt and her special brother, Asa.

The children followed Rembrandt out of the paint world and back into the field where
they had left their red wagon. They reloaded the supplies into the wagon and headed back to the cottage with Rembrandt leading the way. They grew fond of the cat who would forget the children were following her and head out to explore a movement in the bushes. But she always returned to the path and turned around to make sure Asa and Prentiss were okay. Eventually, the threesome made it back to the magic cottage. Asa parked the wagon back under the trees. Prentiss went to retell the day's events to Sherlock, Nikki, and Herbie. Acapella was visiting the castle in the clouds and Morph was working on the mailbox. Herbie wanted to know if the children had painted magic carrots into the circus scene as snacks for the audience. Everyone laughed at this proposal, although Herbie couldn't understand why.

Nikki suggested that the children go for a cool swim in the turquoise-colored pond. It was a very hot day and the Sunflower

Queen was out in full force. Asa and Prentiss agreed that a swim would be refreshing, especially after all the exercise they had had on the trapeze. But it was getting late, and the twins could hear Grammy's dinner bell in the distance.

"We can go swimming tomorrow, Nikki, can't we?" asked Prentiss.

"Of course, darling. Tomorrow it is. Don't forget to pack your swimsuits," Nikki ordered as the children waved goodbye and jumped on the transporter that would take them back to another world of grandparents, soft beds, and warm food. They did not expect for a minute that a dangerous adventure awaited them in the pond.

Chapter Seven
Icthys Pond

Asa and Prentiss remembered to bring their swimsuits the next morning. Fortunately, the Sunflower Queen blessed Serendipity with another gloriously hot, sunny day. When the twins left the transporter, they were eager to go directly to the pond and jump in the luscious, turquoise water. But they remembered Sherlock's scolding yesterday, when they failed to complete their detective duties by looking for clues. Obediently, the children first went to the cottage where Nikki and the others were already soaking in the rays of the sun. It was a bit humorous to see a dog, a squirrel, a butterfly, a rabbit, a bird, and a cat sprawled out on beach towels and wearing sunhats and sunglasses. But, this was Serendipity.

Sherlock pretended to be napping but watched from the corner of his eye to see if the twins would check for clues. His heart skipped a beat with joy when he saw that they did not disappoint him. Asa came back from the birdhouse with an acorn clue. Prentiss found a silky parchment in the mailbox. The twins shared their finds:

"Well, Ace, this clue is strange," said Prentiss. She unfolded the paper and read,

Glub, glub, glub, glub, glub

She added, "Hmm… I remember that sound.. glub… wasn't it in one of our nursery songs that Mommy used to sing to us?"

Asa laughed, "Yep! I think it made us giggle. Well, here's the acorn clue:

Two plus three is what you'll find
The sum occurs within the rhyme
Do not unscramble words you read
Who makes this sound is what you need.
Be careful where you swim today,
Trouble lurks in what some say.

"So," Asa continued, "Two plus three equals five. And there are five glubs that we are not supposed to unscramble."

"Right," agreed Prentiss, "And in the nursery song who made that glub sound? Fish...

And fish live..."

"In the pond," Asa finished his sister's sentence. "And we are going swimming in the pond, but the fish may lead us into trouble. So, we're supposed to keep our eyes open and pay attention to what's happening."

"Bravo! You are great detectives, Asa and Prentiss," cheered Sherlock. "Just remember as you have fun today, that calm waters above are sometimes dangerous below. Be very careful."

"Please be careful," begged Nikki. "I'll wait for you by the large boulders. If you need me, just call. Morph will be watching from above along with Acapella. Rembrandt will not be far away, but cats are not too fond of water. Herbie and Sherlock can't swim. So, please, think before you act."

"We will be fine, Nikki, honest" promised Prentiss. "We don't take unnecessary chances. It's not like a shark lives in those waters!"

Herbie added, "Be prepared for anything in Serendipity. Now eat your carrots!"

The children obeyed, waved goodbye and headed off to the pond. The turquoise blue water was absolutely dazzling in the morning sun. At first the children could not see what all the fuss was about. There was absolutely no sign of life in the pond, except for the gorgeous lily pads floating on top. Asa and Prentiss hid in the bushes surrounding the pond and put on their swimsuits. Just as they were getting ready to dive into the water, Prentiss shouted, "Asa, cut that out!"

Asa answered innocently, "What out? What are you talking about? I didn't do anything!"

"Oh, no? Then how did I get splashed with water!" Prentiss answered while pointing to the streams of cool liquid dripping down her face.

Asa couldn't help but laugh at the sight as much as he tried not to. "Honest, Pren. It wasn't me."

Prentiss questioned, "If not you, then who? Maybe something is down there. I think we better take all our gifts with us just in case."

"I agree," answered Asa. "But first, let's use our carrot powers. Stare at the lily pads and tell me what you get."

Both twins stared at the target. "I see five fish under the pads," Prentiss described her vision. "Two bigger ones and three little ones. That explains the five glubs and the two plus three."

"That's what I see, too," added Asa. "But when I think about the future, all I see is black inky stuff. That couldn't be good."

"Well, we have all our gifts with us. We better take them along, just in case. Let's go. First destination, the lily pads." With that, Prentiss dove into the water. Asa followed behind her. The twins were shocked at how refreshing the water felt against their skin, not too cold or hot. As soon as their green eyes got used to the view underwater, Asa and Prentiss were astonished at what they saw: beautiful plant life in colors of green and yellow, exquisite colorful shells, a carpet of milky white sand, and lots of bubbles coming from under the lily pads. Five sets of bubbles. The children went to investigate.

As they swam closer to the bubbles, they saw five fish pop out from behind some plants. One was a brilliant, dazzling gold; one was jet black; and the three smaller ones were a mixture of the two—a gold and black striped one; a gold speckled one; and one with black spots against gold scales. The three little fish were frightened by their presence and hid behind the plants. The black fish seemed brave and came out to greet the children. Knowing how things were in Serendipity, Asa and Prentiss were not at all surprised when the fish began speaking to them in perfect English:

"Welcome to our home... Icthys Pond. My name is Ebony. Let me introduce my wife, Goldy. Our children are a bit shy, but you will get to know them. Their names are Stripey, Specky, and Spotty."

"Yes, welcome, welcome. We don't get too many visitors. Oh, I almost forgot. You're humans and will need some help breathing and talking under water. Please accept these gifts," Goldy added. She gave each of the children a breathing device so that they could swim for long periods underwater. It also had a built in microphone that allowed them to speak and hear each other underneath the surface.

Asa responded first, "Nice to meet you." He was very excited to be able to breathe and talk underwater. It was a great feeling. "My name is Asa and this is my sister, Prentiss. Did you say Icthys Pond? Something tells me that has something to do with Science."

Stripey came out from behind the plants and said, "Any third grader knows that Icthys is part of the classification for fish."

Goldy reprimanded her son, "Stripey, don't be rude to our guests."

"Yes, mother, I'm sorry," Stripey replied, but it didn't seem like his heart was in the apology.

"Do you go to school?" Asa asked.

"Haven't you ever heard of a school of...oh, I mean, yes. We go to fish school. But it's summer now, and all we like to do is play," answered Stripey. "The problem is that there is no one to play with. We just have each other, and my two sisters get boring."

"Stripey!" Ebony warned. Stripey decided he better not push his parents' fins too far.

At the mention of fun, Specky and Spotty made themselves visible. Introductions went all around. As soon as Asa and Prentiss explained that they were good friends of Nikki, Sherlock, Morph, Herbie, Acapella, and Rembrandt—Goldy and Ebony felt comfortable with the humans.

"I have an idea," said Goldy. "Specky, Spotty, and Stripey, why don't you show our visitors around the pond. Just be careful of the cave at the end. If you can promise to behave, you may go out to play."

"You mean I'm not watered anymore?" asked Stripey excitedly.

Prentiss wondered how a fish gets watered when it lives in a pond. She asked, "Excuse me, but what does it mean to be watered?"

Spotty chimed in, "Oh, Stripey is an expert at being watered!"

Goldy answered, "Getting watered is like human children getting grounded. Do you understand?"

Asa answered, "Oh, yeah, we know what grounded means alright!"

"Stripey, my son, you're still watered. But we will make today an exception due to our visitors. And you will behave, won't you?" said Ebony as more of a command than a question.

"Yes, sir," promised Stripey. "Well, come on, let's go!" Stripey swam around in small circles causing underwater currents as he went.

As soon as they were out of range of their parents, the three little fish began a game of tag, racing around the twins so quickly that their heads spun. Trying not to be a bad hostess, Specky stopped playing and asked the twins to join them. Of course, the humans could not possibly keep up with the fish. Prentiss motioned to Asa to meet her behind a huge plant. She pressed on the ray of her golden locket and wished for two small motors to propel her brother and herself through the water. Asa nodded thanks to his sister as each of them placed the motors on their backs. Specky, Stripey, and Spotty stared in amazement when the boy and girl beat them at their own fish game.

Being a sore loser, Stripey announced, "Let's stop this boring game. I have a better one. It's called, Find the Answer."

Asa was curious, "How do we play?"

"Oh, it's easy," said Stripey innocently, "See that cave over there. Well, we'll all swim over to it and the first one to guess what's inside correctly wins! See? It's easy."

Spotty whined, "Stripey, were all going to get in big trouble. Tell them…"

Stripey swished his tail right into his sister, cutting off her words. "Of course I'll tell them that it is the best game we have and I hope they win. Isn't that what you were going to say, little sister?"

Spotty was afraid to go against her brother and nodded "yes."

"So, what's the catch?" asked Prentiss. "There must be more to this game than that."

Specky, wanting to have some fun herself answered, "That's just it. The fun is in the guessing. Don't worry. We play this game all the time."

"I thought I heard your parents say to stay away from the cave," warned Prentiss.

"Oh, that's a different cave far from here," Stripey lied. "Come on, let's start."

The twins did not trust Stripey and decided to stay close to each other. The five swimmers headed over to the cave. Asa and Prentiss noticed that Spotty and Specky stayed very far behind the others. Stripey gained courage with the humans along for the fun. He swam in big circles around the twins, acting bold in their presence.

Asa and Prentiss cautiously headed toward the opening of the cave. At first, it was so dark inside that they could not see anything. Remembering what they had envisioned when they first looked at the lily pads, the twins wondered if maybe the answer to this riddle was that nothing was in the cave. Suddenly, the murky darkness was interrupted by two huge glowing eyes, erasing the idea that nothing lived inside the underwater cave. In the meantime, Spotty and Specky trembled behind a rock and Stripey blew bubbles at the eyes inside the cave, keeping a distance far behind the twins. The bubbles angered the cave dweller. It now roared forward, revealing eight long tentacles. Asa and Prentiss found themselves face to face with an octopus!

The twins started their little motors and swam as fast as they could away from the cave with the octopus in hot pursuit. Stripey, of course, was far ahead of the twins out of harm's way with his sisters right beside him.

Asa and Prentiss had to think fast, because they could not out swim the monster chasing them. Prentiss took out the ruby feather quill and wrote:

Believe us when we tell you that we want to be friends. We are not here to harm you.

Asa took out the green feather and sang a soothing tune that would calm the octopus while giving him the message written by the quill. The plan worked. When the octopus heard the beautiful music and read the words floating to him in the water, he stopped chasing the children. Then a strange thing happened. The big, scary octopus began to cry, sob in fact.

Asa and Prentiss honestly did not know what to do. They had never been in a predicament like this one. They figured that this creature probably speaks English like everything else in Serendipity. So they tried conversation.

"Mr. Octopus, sir," began Prentiss, "Please don't cry. What is the matter?"

93

The octopus gulped down some tears and replied, "Those fish are always teasing me. They come by my cave and blow bubbles or say mean things and then swim off. They never stay and play. No one will play with me. They look at my eyes and my tentacles and think that I am a mean guy. I'm not really. I'm very kind."

"I'm so sorry," said Asa. "Tell me. If I remember right, an octopus usually doesn't live in a pond. How did you get stuck here in Serendipity?"

"Oh," sniffled the octopus. "It's a long, sad story. I was minding my own business out in the ocean when a fisherman caught me in one of his nets. He didn't want to be responsible for me, so he just dumped me back in the water. The trouble was that I was miles from my home by that time and lost my way. I ended up in a river. The river current pushed me further from the ocean. Then the river ended into a waterfall. I found myself falling for a long time and plopped right into this pond. I have been stuck here ever since. Oh, it wouldn't be so bad except that those three fish drive me crazy. They need to be taught a lesson, especially Stripey."

"Now that's really weird. Don't rivers flow into the sea?" questioned Asa.

"Well, most rivers flow into the sea. But in Serendipity, anything can happen, including rivers that flow away from the ocean," the octopus explained.

"One more thing," Asa added. "I don't remember seeing a waterfall around here. Now that would be so cool!"

"There are many things you haven't seen yet. More than you can experience in one summer," the octopus replied. "But all I want to do is find some friends. I am so lonesome and those bratty fish are so mean to me."

"Well, maybe we can help," said Prentiss. "If I remember correctly, you can produce some black inky stuff, right? What if you make Stripey believe that you captured us in that stuff. He would be quite frightened. Then when we come out and laugh with you, maybe he would get the message. What do you think?"

"Great, Pren," said Asa.

"Wonderful!" shouted the octopus, clapping all his tentacles together.

"Well, before we start, may I ask what we should call you?" asked Prentiss very politely. "We are Prentiss and Asa."

"My name is Cephal O. Pod. My friends, if I had any, would call me Ceph," said the octopus.

"Hi, Ceph. Nice to meet you," answered Prentiss. "Your name is the class for an octopus... your head meeting your feet."

Asa groaned, "Don't worry about her, Ceph. She has a real thing for learning."

"No, no, Asa and Prentiss. That is very interesting. My head does go right into my feet now doesn't it? I am so glad that you are calling me Ceph. Now, let's start the show. I'd love to teach Stripey a lesson he will never forget."

Asa and Prentiss started screaming for help. As soon as Stripey and his sisters swam over to see what was going on, Ceph let out his inky cloud. The three fish were so frightened that they started swimming in circles. Stripey became so dizzy that he fainted onto to the sand bed. Specky and Spotty were crying uncontrollably. In all the commotion, Asa and Prentiss swam out of the dark cloud and showed the girls that they were just fine. They patted Stripey on the dorsal fin until he woke up.

Stripey screamed when he saw the humans. He gasped, "You're... you're okay... you're alive. Did you kill the octopus?"

"No," said Asa. "And you'll be lucky if your father doesn't water you for life when I get through telling him about the little joke you played on us."

"Oh, please don't tell my dad, please," begged Stripey.

Asa knew that the lesson was working. "Well, I won't if you

promise to be nice to Ceph, the octopus. He is really quite nice and just wants friends. And you, Stripey, are going to become the best friend he ever had, aren't you?"

He is really quite nice and just wants friends.

"Oh, sure, yes, you bet. Anything!" pleaded Stripey.

Prentiss held one of Ceph's tentacles and led him out in the open. She made the introductions: "Stripey, Specky, Spotty meet Ceph. Ceph meet you new best friends."

The fish, the twins, and the octopus had a great time together. Ceph pretended to be a merry-go-round. The fish and the children grabbed on to five of the eight tentacles and Ceph spun them around and up and down. They all had a wonderful time. By that time it was getting late. Goldy sent a message to her children, by blowing a large pond snail shell, which commanded the fish to come home.

Before they left, Ceph asked, "Do you promise to come back and play with me?"

Stripey answered, "Well, I should be finished being watered in three days. I will try to be really good so that I don't get in trouble again. After that, my sisters and I will come to play everyday. Oh, and by the way, we are going to have to explain you to our parents. That might take some fast thinking."

Prentiss said, "Why don't you try the truth for once? It works for me."

Everybody started laughing. Stripey promised to tell his parents the whole story, and Specky and Spotty said that they would back their brother up. Ceph waved goodbye to his new friends and went back into the cave for a nap. Asa and Prentiss followed the three little fish and thanked them for a great day. They assured Goldy and Ebony that everything happened just as expected. Now this wasn't exactly a lie… Asa and Prentiss believed that the unexpected was always what was expected in Serendipity. The children promised to come back to the pond. They gave a warning look to Stripey that they would be checking to make sure he followed through with all his promises.

Somehow, the twins felt much older by the end of this day. They had taken on some huge responsibilities down there in the pond, and it felt good. When their heads popped up out of the water, Nikki was waiting for her wards with nice big beach towels in her mouth. The children patted themselves dry and walked with Nikki back to the cottage. Acapella was practicing a song, and Rembrandt was in the middle of an afternoon nap. Sherlock, Herbie, Morph, and Nikki wanted to hear all about the twins' adventures underneath the pond.

The part about the octopus made Herbie so nervous that he fainted. Nikki licked his face until he woke up.

Sherlock beamed with pride at the way the children had handled themselves: "You two have come a long way from childhood. Don't go too far. You still have many years of wonderment to enjoy. Remember, kindness is contagious. Be nice to others and they will return the favor. A creature may look frightening and act mean, but it could be because he is judged by his appearance instead of by his heart and soul. Use your good judgment to think before you act. You chose the right path… you saw the inky water in your carrot vision and you trusted that this would be the right path. You could have chosen to follow that little rascal, Stripey. Instead, it is Stripey who learned right from wrong. Congratulations, Asa and Prentiss. Today it is my honor to present you special medals that read, Detective, First Class. You each have earned it. You are lifelong residents of Serendipity. You may grow old in years, but your wonderful imaginations will always keep you young. Your logic and knowledge will keep you out of harm's way."

Asa asked, "Wow! Detective, First Class. Does this mean school is out? We passed?"

"No, son," answered Sherlock. "You still have a few more adventures here before the summer is through. Very interesting ones, indeed! And don't try to read my mind with your carrot vision, right! It won't work on me unless I want it to work! It's time for you two to go home. Tomorrow is another day."

As Prentiss and Asa gathered their things and walked to the transporter, they thought they saw a yellow blur dashing in and out of the boulders near the pond. The twins were so exhausted that they didn't have the energy to investigate. Even Detectives, First Class need to rest once in a while. They decided to leave this adventure for tomorrow.

Chapter Eight
The Quackers

The twins awoke to rain tapping on their bedroom window. As they walked downstairs to enjoy a wonderful breakfast, they spied Papa rustling papers and mumbling to himself. They guessed he was looking for something.

"Good morning, Papa," said Prentiss giving her grandfather a kiss on the cheek. "Are you looking for something?"

"Good morning, Asa and Prentiss. Yes, I have misplaced my spectacles. Can't read the newspaper without them! Maybe the two of you can help. You seem like first class detectives!" Papa snickered.

Grammy entered the room just as Papa finished his last words. She cleared her throat and tapped Papa on the shoulder, giving him a warning look to hush up. The twins looked at each other a bit shocked as they had just received their First Class Detective badges yesterday and had not shared them with their grandparents, just as they had not showed them any of the gifts they had received.

Papa coughed in embarrassment and kept busily looking for his glasses. Grammy went over to a table by Papa's favorite chair and pulled the spectacles out from behind a cushion. "Here you are! You probably fell asleep with them on yesterday and they fell off your nose! Now, everyone, how about a big breakfast?"

At that moment, the raindrops fell in a tympanic beat upon the windows. Grammy added, "My! Looks like a real storm today. You two better take umbrellas with you before you head out this morning!!"

"No problem, Grammy," said Asa. "We have two with us all the time! Good for bird poop or rain!"

At that remark, Prentiss pushed Asa into the kitchen. He almost fell right into the marmalade and toast, scrambled eggs, crisp bacon, and melon balls that decorated the table. He turned to swat his sister and noticed the look on her face. Asa realized that he shouldn't have mentioned the original purpose of the poop umbrellas, but it was too late to take it back. He shrugged embarrassingly at his sister, quietly took a seat, and began wolfing down his food.

Prentiss decided the best course of action was to sit and eat also. The sooner they finished, the faster they could get on their way before anymore beans were spilled. After they finished the meal, the twins packed up their gear, grabbed the meals Papa prepared, and headed for the imagination transporter. On the way, the twins talked about their grandparents' mentioning the detective business, but they decided it was probably just a coincidence.

Asa and Prentiss arrived in Serendipity in the middle of a thunderstorm. They were happy that they had the umbrellas they had received earlier in their adventures packed neatly with their supplies. The twins simultaneously opened the umbrellas, protecting themselves from the downpour. Quickly, the children ran to the magic cottage. Rembrandt was hiding from the rain, taking a nap on the blue braided rug. Herbie, fearful of catching cold, was concocting a carrot smoothie. Morph flew in circles around the living area until she found a comfortable spot on one of the freshly cut wildflowers sitting in a vase on the entrance table. Acapella was resting in her gold birdcage, exhausted from her performance last night at the music castle in the sky. Sherlock and Nikki were sitting in the blue floral chairs, enjoying a nice chat in front of a crackling fire Nikki had started in the fireplace.

Nikki pranced over to the children as soon as they entered the cottage and said, "Oh, children, you are soaking wet. Take off your wet clothing and wrap yourselves in these towels." Nikki, always prepared, pulled some warm towels from one of the chairs surrounding the dining table and gave them to the children. Then she added, "There, now. Your umbrellas will dry nicely out on the porch. Go put them there and join us by the fire. Serendipity has an emergency situation, one that needs the help of its two newest Detectives, First Class."

The children were elated at the mention of their new titles. Each pulled from their pockets the badges of honor that Sherlock had presented to them yesterday. They followed Nikki's instructions and joined their dog and Sherlock in the living area. The twins curled up on the floor next to the fire.

Sherlock was the first to speak: "Asa and Prentiss, a serious problem has developed. The Quacker children are missing – all five of them. Their mother, Ana Tidae Quacker, is sick with worry. She needs our help! And it is a bit parky today, which will not help in the search!"

Asa and Prentiss took in the terrible news. While Asa was reporting that the twins had seen something yellow streak across one of the boulders yesterday, Prentiss pulled out a paperback dictionary she had added to the supplies. She figured that it might come in handy since many of the names of the creatures living in Serendipity had something to do with school subjects. Between the two of them, the twins were so far able to figure out the names, but now that they were Detectives, First Class, Prentiss worried that the problems were going to become more difficult than before. She thought that the whole situation was very strange, since it was the twins' imaginations making up the experiences in Serendipity. But, many of the ideas were buried deep in their minds, in the space held for dreams that a person doesn't often remember. In any case,

Prentiss was very happy she had the little book with her. She looked up Mother Quacker's name – Anatidae – and discovered it was a family classification for ducks and other waterfowl. She was very satisfied with herself and would later share the information with her brother.

Sherlock's mind was classifying the clues the team had gathered: "Right then… the last time Ana saw her ducklings was about 6 p.m. last night. She tucked them into their nests and went to read the latest edition of *Waterfowl*. When she went to get her children up for breakfast, their nests were empty. That was at 7 a.m. this morning, two hours ago. She has not seen them since. Now, being that they are very young ducklings, we can assume that they woke up hungry. They either found their own breakfast or are very hungry by now. Asa and Prentiss, what do ducks eat?"

Asa thought for a minute and answered, "Ducks are omnivores… they eat plants but they also eat worms, mollusks, and anything else they can find. Since it rained this morning, there might be a lot of worms out."

Nikki beamed with pride. "That was a beautiful analysis, Asa. I am so proud of you!" and with that the dog licked Asa's face from chin to forehead. The boy wiped away the slobber with his shirt sleeve.

Feeling a little left out, Prentiss added, "And their favorite plant food is the tall grass near the pond. I believe that would be an excellent place to begin. And, may I ask, where is the mother in question now?" Prentiss tried to sound very much like one of the police detectives she had seen on television.

Sensing that her girl was in need of a kiss herself, Nikki walked over to Prentiss and said, "Bravo! Prentiss, that was an excellent deduction and a perfect question!" Nikki then gave the girl the same lick-kiss she had given Asa. Prentiss shivered with excitement.

Sherlock answered Prentiss's question: "Ana Quacker went home to look for clues and she should be here at the cottage any minute. She is quite knackered, what, with being up all night."

Just then, the group heard a knock at the door and Morph, who was closest to it, opened it. There stood Ana Tidae Quacker, a beautiful specimen of a waterfowl: orange-yellow perfectly formed webbed feet, a lovely oval shaped bill of the same color, and the softest, fluffiest down-like feathers the children had ever seen. Sherlock introduced Asa and Prentiss to Ana.

The stressed mother was in a tizzy: "Oh, those ducklings cause me such worry. I let them go out to play everyday, and they know full well that they are to come home immediately when they hear me quacking for them. But they are so full of wonderment about the world; they want to know everything! Sometimes it takes me hours to collect all of them! They really are good little ducklings, just a bit too curious for their own good!"

"They really are good little ducklings, just a bit too curious for their own good!"

Prentiss answered, "I am so sorry, Mrs. Quacker. I know children are a big worry to their parents. We have caused some very stressful moments for ours too. Now that we are old and wise, perhaps we can help. We have become pretty good at detective work and would love to solve this mystery. Could you tell us a little about your ducklings, their names perhaps, and something special about each one? It may help with the investigation."

Ana was impressed with the maturity of the twins. As Prentiss spoke, Asa pulled out a pad of notebook paper and a pen. He was ready to take notes! The duck thought carefully, tears coming to her big black eyes as she thought about her ducklings:

"Well, they are quintuplets, you know. So they are very close. Since the two of you are twins, I guess you understand about special bonding!" The twins looked at each other and nodded in agreement. Mrs. Quacker then continued, "But they are very different too. Each one has a unique personality. The oldest is Graham, who has always been independent and who lives for music; next is Saltina, a lovely girl who loves nature; Ani Mal is my artistic duckling; Sesame loves to cook; and the youngest, Wheaton, would swim all day if I let him. Those are my darlings, and although I am very angry at them now for leaving home without permission, I would give anything to see them home safely. Do you think you can help?"

Morph made loving circles around Ana to reassure her that everything would be okay. Nikki put a paw on the distressed mother's wing to let her know that everyone in Serendipity would help find the five missing ducklings. Herbie offered everyone a magic carrot, hoping this would help in the search. Acapella sung sweet melodies to soothe the worried mother, and Sherlock came up with a plan:

"Okay, everyone, we must form search parties. Asa and Prentiss, you two work together because you already have proven how successful you are at solving clues as a team. Nikki, you go ahead and join the twins so you don't worry about their safety. Morph and Acapella can spread the word by air and look around from that heavenly position to see if they can spot the little ducklings. I will notify the fish family and Ceph, the octopus, to be on the lookout for the feathered friends. Then I will stay here with Herbie to act as point person. If you have any news at all, please get word back to me as soon as possible. Herbie, since you are so fast on your feet, you can act as messenger in case news arises. Rembrandt, now where is Rembrandt? Oh, she has probably already taken off on her own for the search. Well, I think that covers it. Any questions?"

Everyone agreed that it was an outstanding plan and assumed their responsibilities. Asa and Prentiss grabbed all their special gifts to help in the search. They realized that this time they would receive no help from clues in the birdhouse or mailbox. They were full fledged Detectives, First Class and would have to rely on their own ingenuity to solve this terrible situation. They only hoped and prayed that the five little ducklings would turn up safe and sound. Prentiss pulled out the magnifying glass she had used so long ago to see if she could spot any webfoot prints anywhere around the cottage. She also found the two rocking horses and asked Asa to turn them into full-sized mounts once again. The twins figured they could cover more ground that way. Nikki helped by carrying the supplies on her back so that the twins would not have any extra weight to slow them down. Each team ate the magic carrots, which made Herbie very happy, and started the search.

Asa had been silent for awhile, but now he spoke to his sister and his dog:

"I think we can go about this search using our wits. Let's think about the way Ana described each of her ducklings. They didn't necessarily stay together. Perhaps that blur of color we saw yesterday, Pren, was the little critters speeding away from home to have adventures of their own. So, what did Ana say about Graham Quacker? Let me check my notes. Ah, here it is: Graham loves music, just like me. Well, if I loved music I know where I would go. I would find a way to get to the castle in the clouds where all the birds hang out. Now, just how would a little duckling manage to fly that high?"

Prentiss answered, "Well, Morph and Acapella didn't help him or they would have said something. What other residents from Serendipity have we met who can fly? Only the frowdinal who took off to meet up with her flock. What if she hung around for awhile? Let's ask the ruby feather quill that will tell us the truth?"

Prentiss pulled out the quill and asked the question, 'Who helped Graham Quacker get to the music castle?'

The pen danced in the sky and then wrote,

Not the frowdinal as you suggest, but a loving bird of green surely did his best.

In unison, Prentiss and Asa shouted, "Johann Sebastian Bird!"

Asa added, "That rascal helped someone else get away from home just as he did many years ago. Let me send him a musical message with the green feather and tell him that if Graham Quacker is at the concert, he is to be sent home immediately in the escort of Morph and Acapella."

Asa pulled out the green feather and sent a tune to Sebastian. He directed the green feather to also send word to Morph and Acapella to go to the castle and meet up with Sebastian. It took less than a minute for the feather to return to Asa with positive news. Graham had been found dancing at the concert in the clouds! Nikki was so excited that she jumped in circles. She ran to Herbie and Sherlock and gave them the good news. Mrs. Quacker fainted from all the excitement, but Nikki licked her bill and brought her around. A moment later, Asa, Prentiss, Nikki, Sherlock, Herbie, and Ana Quacker saw three figures flying in the sky: Morph on one side, Acapella on the other, and Graham Quacker in the middle looking very frightened about the consequences of his misbehavior. When they landed in front of the magic cottage, Sherlock gave Graham a severe scolding.

Ana hugged her duckling and cried, "I don't know whether to shake you or hug you to pieces. Don't ever frighten me like that again!" Then mother and duckling cuddled for a long time.

Prentiss said, "Well, Ace, one down and four to go. Look at your notes and let's see what Ana had to say about the second duckling."

Asa read again from his notes: "Saltina Quacker loves nature. Hmmm... do you think she may have wandered into the grove? Not that I am excited about revisiting that grumpy old tree, but he may know something."

Prentiss chimed in, "You're right, Ace. It's worth a try."

So once again the twins jumped on their rocking-horse steeds and galloped all the way to the grove. This time, however, the grumpy old tree was happy to see his human friends. He had heard about their promotion to Detectives, First Class. The tree yawned and stretched and sent out word to every tree in the grove to look for a little duckling. The twins heard a great deal of rustling above. Soon the old tree spoke,

"You are in luck. We have found Saltina jumping from bush to bush in the groves. The trees have created a strong wind that will blow the little duckling back here any moment."

Just as the giant tree finished talking, the twins felt the effects of a hurricane force wind.

At the end of the commotion, a little ball of fluff landed right in Prentiss's hands. The girl responded, "Well, hello there. Saltina, I presume?"

Saltina was so frightened by the hurricane experience that she couldn't speak. She simply nodded her head.

"Well, Saltina, you have given all of us quite a scare, but especially your mother. She is not too happy with you right now," said Asa sternly.

Prentiss looked at her brother and realized how grown up he sounded, kind of like their dad. The little duck shivered with fear, her little fuzzy yellow feathers standing up on end. The twins led the way on their rocking horses back to the cottage. Mrs. Quacker flew right up to Prentiss's saddle and yanked her duckling daughter to the ground. She gave Saltina a severe scolding and then hugged her tight. Asa and Prentiss nodded at each other and Nikki applauded her young detectives for fine work.

Asa spoke again, "Well, Pren. Time for us to rescue number three duckling. My notes say, 'Ani Mal is creative.' Prentiss, let's see if we can find Rembrandt anywhere. I bet Ani Mal is in the paint world having a grand time."

Prentiss nodded in agreement with her brother. The twins focused on the shuttered windowsill where Rembrandt often took cat naps. Rembrandt was not there, but eating the magic carrots gave them a very clear vision of their feline friend. To their excitement, they saw Rembrandt carrying Ani Mal in her mouth. They were coming home from the paint circus Prentiss had artistically created. Soon the two artists were seen approaching the cottage. The little duckling was frozen with fear, being carried in the jaws of a cat. When Sherlock questioned the little duck about why she ran away, Ani Mal replied, "Oh, I saw elephants and tigers and even humans on the trapeze. Oh, Mama, it was grand!"

Mrs. Quacker warned her daughter to never leave home without permission again, hugged the little duckling who seemed a little remorseful, and tried to thank the cat for her assistance, but Rembrandt nonchalantly stretched and went back to her perch on the windowsill where she fell back to sleep.

Prentiss said to Asa, "We're on a roll! Isn't Sesame Quacker the little duckling who likes to cook?"

Asa answered, "Correct, Pren. So who is always cooking up concoctions around here? Herbie! Let's check out his private stash of carrots that he keeps in the red bucket."

Herbie, hearing his name and carrots mentioned, joined the twins on their walk down to the fence where the red bucket still hung on a hook. At first, the detectives could not see any evidence that

Sesame Quacker had been nearby the carrot garden or the bucket. Then they heard a scratching noise coming from inside the bucket. Carefully, Prentiss lowered the carrots and bucket off the nail. She removed one carrot at a time and there on the bottom was a very tiny, very full, and very frightened duckling. Asa said, "Sesame Quacker, is that you?"

The little duckling spoke with giant tears rolling down her bill: "I have a terrible headache in my tummy. I want my mama and I want to go home. Ooh, it hurts!"

Ana Quacker quickly waddled over to the fence when she heard her duckling making a fuss. Ana, Prentiss, Asa, Nikki, and Herbie laughed at the site of the little duckling rolling on the ground, her stomach round with the many carrots she had consumed. Mrs. Quacker lovingly swaddled her duckling in her wings and said, "Well, I guess you punished yourself, Sesame. We can fix up your tummy and then we will have a long chat about what happens to little ducklings who leave home without permission."

Asa and Prentiss were exhausted but did not want to stop their work now, with just one duckling left missing. According to Asa's notes, Wheaton loved to swim—not unusual at all for a duckling. They called on their friends the fish and Ceph to see if they could turn up any clues. Prentiss and Asa put on their little motors to help them swim and the breathing/talking devices that Goldy had given them and dove into the turquoise pond water.

When the twins arrived at the bottom of the pond, they saw all the fish enjoying a merry-go-round ride with Ceph. The twins counted six riders – Goldy, Ebony, Stripey, Specky, Spotty, and a fluffy yellow ball, Wheaton. Ceph immediately stopped the ride when he saw his human friends. They explained the situation and Ceph hooked Wheaton on his tentacle and launched him up to the surface of the pond. There, Sherlock fished him out of the water and Mama Quacker grabbed her last duckling covering her youngest offspring with kisses.

Everyone was exhausted that day in Serendipity, except for Rembrandt who seemed to take the day's adventures in her stride. The five little ducklings were back home with their mother and Sherlock devised collars with bells attached that would warn Ana whenever one of her offspring were trying to go off on an adventure. Asa and Prentiss gathered up their belongings and headed for the imagination transporter. They couldn't wait to get back to Papa and Grammy's house where they could enjoy a nice hot meal and cozy beds. The twins discovered many things that day: the fears and joys of being a parent, the belief most offspring seem to hold that nothing bad could ever happen to them, and the wonderful feeling that happens when Detectives, First Class solve cases that help others become reunited with their families. In fact, the twins decided there was no better feeling in the world.

After the brother and sister discussed their day's adventures, they said, "Good-night" to each other and became lost in their own thoughts. As she fell asleep, Prentiss thought about how terrible it is to lose something. She remembered one of her old friends she had lost many years ago, Pink Teddy, and wondered if she would ever see her favorite stuffed pal again. A tear fell from her emerald eyes as she remembered how she carried her friend around the house, often dragging Teddy by one ear. The toy never seemed to complain but seemed especially happy when the girl whispered baby talk in her ear and hugged Teddy so tightly that it looked like every seam would pop. Prentiss drifted off to sleep saying, "Teddy, Pink Teddy, where did you go? I miss you... I love you ..."

Chapter Nine
Pink Teddy

After they kissed Papa and Grammy goodbye the next morning, Asa and Prentiss walked silently up to the imagination transporter. Both twins seemed to be occupied by their own thoughts. Finally, Asa broke the silence, "Pren, you seem very quiet this morning. And you had a rough night. I heard you tossing and turning and calling out for Pink Teddy. Can I help you with anything?"

"Oh, Ace," cried Prentiss. "I can't stop thinking about my Pink Teddy. Remember her? Oh you must. You still have your Blue Teddy. Grammy got them as gifts when we were born. I used to drag Pink Teddy with me everywhere. And then one day, I left her somewhere. I don't remember. So what happens to the toys we lose or outgrow? Do they have their own place like Serendipity?"

Asa put his arm soothingly around his sister's shoulder and said, "Oh, Pren. I do remember Pink Teddy. I haven't played with Blue Teddy since I was a toddler, but Mommy still keeps him up on a shelf in our playroom. I haven't thought about our Teddies in years. I wish I could answer your questions. When we get to Serendipity, let's ask Sherlock. He is so wise; I bet he can tell us something. Maybe it's not too late to find your lost friend. After all, we are pretty good detectives. We solved five missing duckling cases just yesterday!"

Prentiss loved the way her brother could make her feel better when she was feeling down. He had a gift for raising people's spirits. As long as she could remember, Asa was the charmer who could bring a smile to anyone's face. Prentiss thought that she was the serious one; always thinking about some worldly problem to solve. They were both great problem solvers in their own ways. Together, they seemed to have greater powers than either of them separately; two unique individuals with a special bond that made them inseparable. She felt better already knowing that her brother would not let her down. He would help her find answers to her questions, even if it took the rest of the summer. She loved her brother with all her heart.

Asa hated to see his sister so down. She had such an incredible mind that could raise a million questions in minutes. He loved that about her; no stone left unturned. When he thought he had solved a problem, Prentiss would come up with a hundred more, "But, what if's…" She was like deep waters underneath a beautiful, calm surface. And in those mysterious places her imagination bubbled over and her creativity loomed. When that happened, she would stick with a problem until she solved it. She was the artist, the thinker, and the great problem-solver. He vowed to make her happy again if it took the whole summer and many more to come.

Nikki noticed immediately that something was troubling Asa and Prentiss. They walked to the magic cottage slower than usual, their usually bright faces covered in dark storms. "Children, my darlings, what is it?" whined Nikki in the voice she used whenever she fretted over her wards.

Asa answered for them both, "Nikki, do you remember Pink Teddy, Pren's special bear?"

Nikki laughed warmly, "How could I not? She dragged that bear all over the place, her chubby hands clutching on to it for dear life. Oh, my, fond memories. What happened to her? I haven't seen her in years."

"That's the problem, Nikki," explained Asa. "We don't know what happened to Pink Teddy. She just disappeared."

Prentiss finally composed herself enough to join the conversation, "Nikki, I was wondering. What happens to old toys? Where do they go? Do they have a special place like Serendipity?"

By this time Sherlock had joined the group. "Good questions, me girl. Remember, children, Serendipity is your creation. If you wish to create a place for old and lost toys, you just need to think it. I am sure in all the commotion yesterday you forgot this little detail. You have all the tools now and all the gifts to make anything appear. Did you forget about your golden locket?"

Instinctively, Prentiss reached for the locket that she always wore around her neck. She had completely forgotten about its powers. Part of her yearned to wish Pink Teddy to appear. But another part was fearful that she had abandoned her bear and that the toy would be angry with her. She walked away from the others to do some soul searching. Never in her life had she run away from the truth. She owed it to herself to discover what had happened to Teddy. She sat down in the red wagon and clutched her golden locket.

Immediately, Pink Teddy appeared in the wagon. She looked pretty much the same: the color of cotton candy, as soft as Grammy's velour throw rugs, black button eyes. The only change Prentiss could see was that a gold scarf was wrapped around Pink Teddy's neck instead of the satin pink ribbon the toy used to wear. Prentiss hugged the bear with all her might and wondered how she would ever discover the adventures the bear had experienced over the past few years.

The only change Prentiss could see was that a gold scarf was wrapped around Pink Teddy's neck instead of the satin pink ribbon the toy used to wear.

Asa came to his sister's rescue. He walked over to the wagon and pulled the purple ball out of his pocket. The brother held the orb above Pink Teddy's head and wished for the bear to be able to use her five senses. Instantly, the stuffed animal began to move her tiny mouth. As she looked around and spotted Prentiss, alligator sized tears welled in her button eyes.

"Prentiss, is that you, is it really you?" cried the bear. "I thought I had lost you forever. Of course, you are much bigger than I remember, and you finally managed to learn to walk I see. But those emerald eyes and crooked smile… they haven't changed at all. Please forgive me! I am so sorry I lost you in the airport that day on the way to Alaska with your parents."

Prentiss could not hold back the tears. She sobbed for minutes, creating such heartbreak, that Nikki, Sherlock, Herbie, Morph, and Acapella started weeping too. Looking closely, Asa noticed that even Rembrandt had a tear in her eye, although she tried not to show it. Prentiss gulped and said, "Teddy, do you think you lost me? Why, all these years I thought I was careless and lost you. What happened?"

"Oh, no, my girl. Your little chubby hand held on to me for dear life. We were all inside the airport, waiting for a flight to Alaska. Asa was holding Blue Teddy and you, as I said, had me. The two of you were sitting in your twin stroller, do you remember? It was charcoal grey with orange trim, and the two of you sat side-by-side."

Prentiss said, "I don't remember sitting in the stroller, but there are tons of pictures of us in it."

"Well, anyway," continued Pink Teddy, "Prentiss, you were babbling to me as you usually did. I remember that we passed a toy shop inside the airport. You didn't notice at all between talking gibberish to me and patting Asa on the head. But I saw giant toys the likes of which I had never seen. I tried to wriggle my way out of your hand so that I could roll over to the shop and take a look. I thought that I would only be gone a minute. Prentiss, Asa reached over and gave you one of his famous kisses. You turned to him to return the favor. When you turned, you let go of me. I was on the edge of the stroller and I used the momentum of your jiggling to bounce out onto the floor. You didn't notice, nor did Asa or your parents. Besides, the two of you couldn't say too many English words yet. I figured that I would catch up with you in a few minutes.

"I rolled over to the toy store and stared in amazement at giant polar bears, tigers, lions, elephants and monkeys. Oh, they were grand!! Some of them could speak if you pushed on their stomachs. I could have watched for hours. By the time I realized how long I had been in the store, it was too late. All of you had moved on. A salesperson saw me on the floor and picked me up. She thought I had fallen off the sales rack so she tossed me on to the top of the pile. I didn't know what to do.

"I was stuck in the store for days. I kept hoping by some miracle that you would come strolling into the store. But, of course, that never happened. Well, one day, a little girl with golden curls and blue eyes lifted me up and cuddled me in her arms. Now of course, she wasn't as good a hugger as you, Prentiss, but it did feel great to have that human touch again."

Prentiss tugged on her hair, like she did whenever she was put out by something. Asa knew that his sister was jealous of the blonde girl who caught Teddy's attention. He tried to make his twin feel better, "I bet she didn't love you as much as Pren either, huh Pink Teddy?"

"I doubt anyone ever could," said Pink Teddy. "I still loved you too, Prentiss, but I was so lonely. Well, I heard the child begging her parents to buy me. I tried to explain that I belonged to you Prentiss, but of course, the humans couldn't hear me. I thought that the little girl understood, but she wanted me so badly that she never would have said anything. Well, I decided that being with another human was better than being alone on the top of a sales rack.

"The child's parents finally gave in and bought me. There was some commotion about my price as I had no tag and there were no other Teddies like me. I was a bit offended when the store sold me for $5. I know I was worth much more than that! The girl, Sophie was her name, cuddled me tightly. I traveled with her to her home in Europe… yes, Europe. She lived in London, England. It's quite beautiful there; you should visit someday. Lots of castles! Well, I had to get used to the different accent. Why, everyone sounded like Mr. Sherlock, come to think of it. Anyway, I lived with Sophie for three years. I had a good life with the girl. She invited me to many tea parties and hardly ever got me dirty." Eying the sadness in Prentiss's eyes, Teddy added, "Of course, her parties weren't as much fun as the good times we had together, Prentiss. Anyway, time passed quickly.

"Then one day, Sophie decided to give me away. She placed me in a dark bag with some other things and I ended up in a children's hospital. Another little girl, recovering in the hospital, became my human. She had red hair and brown eyes and her name was Harriet. I was happy to see Harriet through some sick times. Poor thing, she was stuck in the hospital for weeks. When she was better, her parents took us on a trip to the United States. In honor of her getting well, Harriet's parents bought me a beautiful gold scarf to replace the pink ribbon that had become quite tattered through the years. I thought, maybe I would see you again someday. But Harriet took me to the library one day and left me on a shelf. I was alone once again. Someone lifted me off the shelves and threw me in the trash. Imagine the embarrassment to end up in a trash can!

"The next thing I knew, I was sitting up in a cloud in Serendipity. It is a nice cloud filled with used up toys. We all sit around talking about our adorable children and the good times we had. Each one of us can see our humans as they grow up and watch all their experiences until they become adults. I've rather enjoyed watching you and your brother through all the adventures you've had over the past few days."

Prentiss asked, "But how did you get to Serendipity? This is very hard to understand."

Sherlock tried to explain, "Right, so it is, girl! The imagination is a tricky thing. The more one uses it, the stronger it gets. You've witnessed this for yourselves this summer. Once you stretched your ability to imagine, old experiences you have had came rushing in to the space. Without thinking too hard about it, your mind helped you create what you remembered about one of your favorite toys, Pink Teddy."

"And last night I went to bed thinking of Teddy," continued Prentiss.

"Boy, did she ever!" added Asa. "She was yelling, 'Pink Teddy, Pink Teddy, where are you?' all night long."

Sherlock said, "Exactly! Prentiss, your thoughts were so strong that Pink Teddy materialized on the Lost Toy Cloud. The rest you know."

"Then this morning, something strange happened," said Pink Teddy. "I was looking down at you when all of the sudden I popped up in the red wagon. And there you were! Oh, Prentiss, it has been such a long, long time. But my love for you, my first child, never was lost. You gave me my heart and I will always love you for that. And now, I see you never forgot me either. I have been in your heart, your mind, even your dreams! At last, dear girl, we are together again!"

For a long time, Prentiss could not speak. She tried to replay that day in the airport when she was not even walking yet. But her mind was fuzzy and she couldn't quite get a good picture of that experience. She could remember snapshots of the moment: Holding Teddy, speaking to her, smothering the pink bear with baby kisses. But so much time had passed. Prentiss, the deep thinker, wondered if childhood memories fade over time and eventually disappear. Then she remembered that Papa and Grammy were very old and they still could tell stories about things that happened when they were very small children. It all started to make sense, what Papa and Grammy said, why Asa and she were in Serendipity, and the importance of keeping a healthy imagination.

Asa looked at her with knowing eyes. Prentiss knew her twin was thinking similar thoughts. They were enjoying a very special gift that summer in Serendipity, the gift of childhood. It was a special time when clouds could become soft fluffy lands holding music castles in their folds; where wildflower landscapes could hide new canvases waiting to be painted by young, imaginative artists; where seemingly calm ponds masked a busy life far below the surface; and large granite-top boulders hid mischievous ducklings looking for paths to unknown adventures. Most of all, Asa and Prentiss thought about the many new friends they met and the new understanding they discovered about the love their pet, Nikki, had for them.

Each one of the group was lost in thought when Herbie let out a terrible scream.

"What is it, Herbie?" asked Nikki.

Herbie was so shaken that he could hardly speak. "I got so choked up over the story that I went to get a tissue to wipe my eyes and blow my nose. I ate a carrot on the way. As I was passing by the mailbox, my paw touched the top. A terrible vision came into view, terrible I say. Oh, my, my, my…I hope it's not too late. Poor Morph!"

"What are you talking about?" shouted Sherlock. "Pull yourself together and tell us!" The others all looked around and noticed that Morph was nowhere in sight.

Herbie wiped his nose and whiskers. "Morph has been caught in the web of a spider. If we don't help her soon, she will become dinner for that horrible creature!"

"What spider? Where?" shouted Asa.

Pink Teddy spoke up. "I think I know. I brushed that tree over there on my way down to the red wagon. I saw a huge spider web with something purple struggling to get out. I didn't think much about it at the time. I was too busy wondering what was happening to me!

Is this Morph creature purple by any chance?"

Prentiss picked Pink Teddy up so that his eyes met hers. "Yes, Teddy. She is purple. Quick, show us where you saw the tree. Take us there. Here, get on my shoulders and give us directions!"

Prentiss and Pink Teddy led the way into the grove. They quickly explained to the grumpy tree what had happened and he pointed to a young tree about fifty feet from his roots. The rescue squad reached the tree. Morph looked desperate. Her beautiful wings were covered with strong silky fibers. Her legs tried to wriggle free.

Once again Herbie fainted, for the scene was just too much for him. Nikki licked the rabbit's face while Prentiss lifted Pink Teddy up as high as she could, until the bear's arms touched the web. Pink Teddy worked hard removing the chainlike strings from Morph's body. The bear spoke soothingly to Morph to reassure her.

When the butterfly was almost free, a dark shadow spread over the web. The spider was returning. Sherlock scampered up the tree to talk to the spider. "Say, there! It seems there has been a terrible mistake. Our friend, Morph, has fallen into your web. We are freeing her now, but we certainly don't want you to go hungry. Please follow us home and we will provide you with enough food to last you for a week. There are plenty of insects around our wildflowers and we will help hunt them for you if you wish."

The spider nodded in agreement and Sherlock made his promise good. Morph recovered quite nicely as well as Herbie. Pink Teddy was a true hero. Prentiss thought she understood how a mother must feel when her child wins a contest in school! The inhabitants of Serendipity spent the rest of the day partying.

Asa asked his sister, "Isn't it strange? We didn't get any gifts today, did we?"

Prentiss replied, "We did! We got the best gift… we learned how to find old memories and friends."

The twins had created a beautiful world where lost memories could be found and new ones were created. Although Pink Teddy could not return to Papa and Grammy's house with the twins, she could stay forever in Serendipity. For the rest of the summer, Prentiss summoned her bear as soon as she arrived in Serendipity on the imagination transporter. They had great times together. Pink Teddy helped solve many clues the twins found in the birdhouse and mailbox and she was eventually awarded the badge of Detective, In Training. Life was good and the summer passed quickly. There was time for just one more adventure in Serendipity for Asa and Prentiss.

Chapter Ten
CeeCee

The summer days were growing short and the twins knew they had only a short time left with Papa and Grammy and their friends in Serendipity. So many wonderful adventures had already occurred that Prentiss and Asa could not imagine what else could possibly happen. Then they remembered that Serendipity was their creation and that meant anything could happen.

On the last day of their vacation, Asa and Prentiss rushed through breakfast and goodbyes so that they could spend as much time as possible in Serendipity. When they reached the magic cottage, they found Sherlock, Nikki, Morph, and Herbie looking up at the roof of the cottage. Something new had appeared there overnight and there was much conversation about its meaning and purpose.

Asa joined the group and asked, "What is it? What are all of you staring at?"

Sherlock answered, "Don't you see it, boy? Look, up there on the roof. It's a weathervane in the shape of a whale."

Asa looked up and spotted a cobalt blue whale sticking out of the roof. Below it were letters labeling the four directions, North, South, East and West. The whale was magnificent, edged in gold, but Asa wondered when he or his sister had imagined this new fixture into their unique imaginary world. "Pren, is this your creation?"

Prentiss shrugged her shoulders. "I don't think so. This looks like something you would imagine. What would a weathervane be doing here anyway?"

Sherlock enjoyed the opportunity to open his classroom one last time for the twins. "Ah, good question, Prentiss. Right, well weathervanes date back to Ancient Greece. The first known one came from Athens as a matter of fact. The figures that go on top of the vane usually tell a story about the people or the area. So, I imagine that one of you has a desire to go to sea!"

"We both love the ocean," replied Asa. "And we love to go fishing, too."

"Actually," added Prentiss, "Ever since Pink Teddy described her adventures, I've been dreaming about visiting Europe and especially England. So, maybe I did have a part in this new addition to our world."

Sherlock added, "Now the question is, how does this weathervane work?"

Asa was a bit taken aback that Sherlock had a question. He thought the great detective from Scotland Yard knew everything. "Well," said the boy, "We could use some of our gifts to find out. The ruby quill pen only writes the truth, so that might help."

"Good thinking, Ace," said Prentiss. "Now just how are we going to get up there to find out?"

"Well," answered Asa, "We can use the golden locket to give us wings and the purple ball to make them big enough to help us fly."

The twins carried out their plan and flew up to the top of the roof with beautiful golden wings.

The twins carried out their plan and flew up to the top of the roof with beautiful golden wings. Nikki couldn't help noticing that her twins looked like angels flying through the sky. Once up on the roof, Asa and Prentiss used the quill pen to ask the question about the whale. But to their amazement, the whale spun around and spoke directly to the twins:

"Good morning, young humans. I am Ceta Cea a mammal just like you."

This introduction cued Prentiss to look up Ceta Cea in her dictionary. She discovered that this was a scientific classification for whales, a fact that came as no surprise to the young researcher. The twins introduced themselves and their friends down below on the ground.

Asa asked, "Just what adventures can you provide for us, Ceta Cea."

"Oh please just call me CeeCee; all my friends do. Well, when you spin me around, my nose will point to one of the directions on the weathervane. You can then visit any country in that direction. It is really quite educational. Oh, you must be wondering how you will get there. I will carry you on my back, of course. I can travel through the sky or through the seas, makes no difference to me. We can have a wonderful time!"

Asa grimaced, "I guess I should have paid more attention during Geography."

"Quite!" answered CeeCee. "But it is never too late to learn. I am sure you can think of something to wish for that could help you with geography, now can't you?"

"Of course!" Prentiss said excitedly. "All we need is a globe." With that Prentiss clutched the golden locket one last time and a beautiful gemstone covered globe appeared. Each country was carefully sculpted out of a different gem, the various oceans and seas created from the richest of blue gems, lapis lazuli. The twins took a few moments to search the different countries waiting to be explored.

"But, CeeCee," whined Asa, "We don't have much time left in this summer. Can we have a sneak peek?"

"Why, of course, son," answered the great whale. Just place your finger on the globe and close your eyes. The twins took turns pointing to different countries. Each time they closed their eyes and felt a spinning sensation. Vivid images passed through their creative minds as they visited China, Japan, Bolivia, Chile, Norway, Sweden, Hungary, and France. The twins' desire to have more adventures made them dizzy with delight.

Their explorations halted suddenly when they heard Nikki's loving voice, "I hate to ruin your fun, darlings. But it is almost time for you to say your final goodbyes and return home to your parents. They miss you so and it is almost time for school to begin."

Asa thought that this year in third grade he would pay particular attention to Geography lessons. The children reluctantly put the globe away and thanked CeeCee for the great sneak at what adventures awaited them in future summers. "You will be here next summer, won't you CeeCee?" asked Prentiss.

"If you imagine me, I will certainly be here waiting to take you to many new lands."

"Can we travel by ship?" asked Asa eagerly. "I love ships and pirates and treasure."

"Anything you imagine," repeated CeeCee.

The twins hugged CeeCee goodbye and used their golden wings to fly back down to the ground. Leaving all their friends and the magic cottage was painful. But they took hope in the fact that they would never forget Sherlock, Acapella, Herbie, Morph, or even Rembrandt. As long as they carried these friends in their hearts and souls they could imagine them back to life in Serendipity next summer.

Asa and Prentiss felt happy when they realized that Nikki would be waiting for them at home. However, they would never see their trusted pet exactly the same way. She was special, their personal protector, and a loving creature. The twins knew that whenever she would bark from now on, she would be trying to communicate something to her children.

Thinking about home, the children became homesick for their parents, their friends, and their own rooms. As much as they loved their time with their grandparents, they missed the warm hugs and kisses they shared with their mother and father. Asa and Prentiss knew it was time to leave Serendipity. They took one last long look around, gathered all their gifts, and boarded the imagination transporter for the final time that summer.

They were soon back at Papa and Grammy's house. But this day was different. When they stepped off the transporter, their grandparents were waiting for them at the bottom of the hill. Grammy held a beautiful burgundy velvet sack with gold embroidered letters that read,

The Adventures of Asa and Prentiss in Serendipity
Summer of their Eighth Year
The Magic Cottage

The children were aghast to realize their grandparents knew the name of their special imaginary world.

Asa blurted out, "But, how did you... when did you?"

"Hush, child," said Grammy lovingly. "Did you forget who told you about going up to the hill and using your imaginations? We have visited Serendipity many summers as children. Your parents did too in their time. Now it is your time. Oh, the inhabitants aren't exactly the same. And I am sure the magic cottage changes a bit throughout time, but I bet old Sherlock hasn't changed a bit. Morph must be getting on in years, but she still probably makes a wonderful guardian angel. Herbie must be as nervous as ever. You have images of these magical beings, because we have planted their thoughts through our stories we have told you since you were babes. The others, well, they come from your beautiful imaginations."

"So, you made the yellow truck come to us, Papa?" asked Asa.

"No, not quite," explained Papa. "You thought of the yellow truck and your wish for it to appear and move came to me. One minute it was there in the yard, and the next it was on its way to you where it plopped under the purple ball waiting for you to make it life-sized."

"And you knew we would make up magic carrots and music castles in the sky and the paint world! You knew these things would happen?" cried Prentiss.

"No. You created the ideas, you imagined everything. Your thoughts came to us after. We really got a kick out of the poop umbrellas," chuckled Grammy.

Then Papa added, "Come on kids. Let's load your special gifts into this beautiful sack that Grammy has been sewing for you all summer. Your special souvenirs will be waiting for you next summer when you return. Nothing like keeping everything in its place. Then they don't get lost."

After all their treasures were safely packed, their grandparents showed the twins a special door outside their bedroom that they never noticed before. It had a gold doorknob and gold hinges. Grammy removed a giant golden key from a rope around her neck and unlocked the door.

"When did this get here?" asked Asa. "I never noticed it before?"

"Did we think up this door, too?" added Prentiss.

Grammy said, "No, the door has always been there, but we've kept it invisible so that your curious minds wouldn't get you interested in what lies behind it. We wanted you outside and in Serendipity. But now, you are ready to see what has been part of this family for many generations."

Grammy opened the door revealing a mountain of pure white stairs. The grandparents and children climbed their way up and stood at a landing that ushered them into a huge attic that seemed larger than their grandparents' entire house. The children were amazed to see dozens of other velvet sacks placed carefully on white shelving, each bag embroidered with golden letters identifying the youth who had journeyed to Serendipity throughout the years. They wanted to look inside each sack, but Papa and Grammy told Asa and Prentiss that those memories of the past could not be disturbed. They were the private property of the children who dreamed them. Asa and Prentiss placed their burgundy sack on an empty shelf, noticing that there was plenty of room for them to add velvety bundles in future years.

"And these shelves, Asa and Prentiss, are for your memories...your velvet bag memoirs," Grammy said as she wiped a tear from her eyes.

The children beamed with love for their grandparents. They were sure now that they each had some special genie powers. How else could they explain the amazing adventures they had experienced this past summer? Their incredible youthful minds were filled with thoughts of magic and wondered if they shared special powers with their grandparents.

That night, as they fell asleep for their final time that summer at their grandparents' home, Asa and Prentiss shared the thoughts and dreams of their future adventures in Serendipity. They wondered where CeeCee would transport them and imagined worlds of vast seas, exotic creatures, and sunken treasures.

They wondered where CeeCee would transport them and imagined worlds of vast seas, exotic creatures, and sunken treasures.

The twins could almost taste the saltwater on their lips and the warm ocean breezes on their skin. And just before the Sunflower Queen rose in the morning sky, the children saw themselves sailing off to sea with Nikki, Sherlock, Morph, Acapella, Herbie, CeeCee and even Rembrandt traveling with them. They wondered where they would land, but that would be another summer and another story.